Bad Girl Blvd

Part 3

Buy

for Melodrama

Bad Girl Blvd

Part 3

Bad Girl Blvd 3. Copyright © 2014 by Melodrama Publishing. All rights reserved. No part of this book may be
used or reproduced in any manner whatsoever without
written permission except in the case of brief quotations
embodied in critical articles or reviews. For information,
address Melodrama Publishing, P.O. Box 522, Bellport,
NY 11713.

www.melodramapublishing.com

Library of Congress Control Number: 2014910884
ISBN-13: 978-1620780633
ISBN-10: 1-62078-063-1
Mass Market Edition: March 2016

Interior Design: Candace K. Cottrell
Cover Design: Candace K. Cottrell
Model Photo: Marion Designs

Printed in Canada

Also By

Erica Hilton

Prologue

It was cold outside like Antarctica. White flakes started to cover the windshield of the black Escalade that Phaedra sat in, parked outside of Brookdale Hospital. It was early evening, and the gloomy weather matched her foul mood.

Phaedra didn't know what to do with herself. At first she felt lost and used. Then heartbroken. She gripped the loaded .45, the betrayal clogging her mind and the tears streaming down her face. She had the urge to break something. She had lost so much—Kool-aid, friends, her dignity, and now Clyde and Luca.

***

It had been a week since Clyde had awakened from his coma and called out Luca's name. *What the fuck!* was the first thing that screamed through Phaedra's mind. She was shocked by his choice. She could still remember how before he'd made his choice he looked Phaedra dead in her eyes and dismissed her when, only hours earlier, they had made sweet, passionate love at his home.

Phaedra had been dumb enough to think that they actually had something. But he played her; used her for some pussy. She had finally opened her heart to a man, and within hours he had crushed it. He wanted Luca. He made his choice, and she abruptly left the room, leaving them alone. Phaedra was so confused, because she had so much love and respect for Luca, who had brought her out of the pits of the jungle and bettered her life. The upset and the treachery by her boss tore Phaedra apart. She knew if Kool-aid was still alive he would tell her that she done bumped her fuckin' head and was wildin' the fuck out. Kool-aid was real like that. He spoke the truth to her, and most times she would listen to him. She missed him already. She needed her best friend in her life.

***

Whiteness started to cover the ground and Phaedra's truck. The weatherman had predicted up to four inches of snow. She sat behind the wheel looking detached, pistol in hand. Her mind was spinning out of control with so many things. It felt like she was going crazy.

After two hours of sitting and waiting, watching the snow fall, and feeling the cold take over her soul, Phaedra finally spotted Luca's pearl-white Benz slowly ease into an open parking spot. As Luca parallel-parked, Phaedra keenly watched her and hyped herself up to do the unthinkable. She planned on sliding behind Luca and squeezing two bullets into the back of her head. She would leave her Escalade running with the keys in the ignition and make a fast getaway before Luca's body fell to the ground. Voices in her head kept trying to tell her, "Don't do it. Walk away," but Phaedra shook them off.

Phaedra was burning with jealousy as she watched Luca strut across Linden Boulevard with her black mink coat sweeping the ground, knee-high boots, and a neon blue wig against her pale skin. She gazed down at her own attire—tight jeans, a dark hoodie, ski jacket, and sneakers.

She closed her eyes briefly and took a deep breath. "Just do it," she told herself as Luca neared the entrance to the hospital. It was now or never. Gripping the gun tightly and scowling, she opened the door and stepped out into the cold and snow.

The weather didn't bother Phaedra, her adrenaline running high. With stealth, she moved behind Luca, who was unaware of the threat. She moved closer, her arm outstretched with the barrel of the gun aimed at the back of Luca's head, her finger on the trigger. Her heart started to beat rapidly. It seemed like it was just the two of them on the street and time had stood still.

Just fuckin' do it, Phaedra screamed in her mind. The more she hesitated, the more she felt herself backing out of it and allowing Luca to live.

Phaedra proceeded forward, frowning heavily as the snow covered her face. The snow flurries were everywhere, becoming thicker by the minute, and the ground felt

11

frozen and slippery. Phaedra rushed toward Luca, and just as she was about to pull the trigger, she heard, "Police! Put the gun down! Drop it!"

Luca spun around and became wide-eyed seeing Phaedra pointing a gun at her. She was speechless, frozen with shock.

"Drop the fuckin' gun!" one officer shouted. "Don't fuckin' move!"

Phaedra found herself surrounded by uniformed cops, their guns trained on every part of her anatomy.

Luca and Phaedra locked eyes. There were no words.

Phaedra felt like she could still pull the trigger—take her boss' life and be done with it.

"You ready to go there?" Luca managed to say coolly. Even with a pistol aimed at her, she didn't flinch or panic.

Phaedra didn't say a word. She lowered the gun, and the moment she did so, she was tackled by NY's Finest and thrown against the ground. They twisted her arms behind her, and with a cop's knee in her back and snow in her face, she was placed under arrest.

Luca stood there watching it all take place. In that moment she knew things would never be the same between her and Phaedra.

Phaedra didn't say a single word as she was ushered to the marked police car and shoved into the backseat. She didn't know how the cops became aware of her plan, but it all seemed like a nightmare playing inside her head.

I wanna wake up now, she said to herself. *I wanna wake up now.*

Chapter 1

Clyde sat still in his hospital bed recovering from his gunshot wounds. What were the odds that he had survived two attempts on his life? Well, the second shooting he was saving Luca's life and was willing to die so she would live. It was crazy of him. He'd responded without even thinking. One minute he was caught up in a jam, having cheated on his girl with her best friend, the next he had several hot slugs pumped into his body.

His mouth felt dry, his body ached, and he felt numb in a few places. He still couldn't feel his legs. He had thirty-two staples running from his chest to his pelvis from a life-saving surgery. The bullets had carved a devastating path, causing his lungs to collapse and damaging both kidneys and his spleen. The doctors had told him that, even with months of physical therapy, it may take him years to walk again, since one of the bullets had nicked one of his nerve endings.

Clyde didn't want to believe it. He refused to accept being confined to a wheelchair for the rest of his life. "No,

I will walk again," he'd said defiantly. "I will not live like this forever. I will fucking walk within a year."

His doctor responded, "I understand your determination, and I do appreciate your tenacity, but you need to be realistic. You've suffered severe damage. We warn you not to put too much pressure on yourself."

Clyde frowned. The doctors didn't know shit. He had been shot before in Baltimore and had come back from it. He wasn't going to become a cripple.

His condition was a gruesome sight for his own eyes. He couldn't move, and he'd dropped more than fifty pounds. There was nothing more humbling than a grown man having to rely on nursing staff to bathe him and change his shit bags. Sometimes the unbearable pain only added to his depression and anxiety. It felt like hell, but he was determined to get through it once again.

Dr. McMinn left the room to see about his other patients on the floor. He was supposed to be the best. They called him the miracle man. It was a miracle that Clyde had survived his surgery. He would have to spend a few more weeks recovering in the hospital and then endure months of physical therapy.

Clyde closed his eyes and tried to get some rest. He wished it was all a nightmare he could wake up from, but the pain that surged through his body and the tubes running into him told him otherwise.

***

Luca walked into the room to see Clyde with his eyes closed and assumed he was asleep. She went near his bedside and touched his hand. He looked like hell, but at least he was still alive. She pulled the chair next to his bed, removed her mink coat and placed it behind her, and sat silently near him. She sighed heavily, feeling ambivalent. Clyde had sacrificed his own body to save her life, but he had also cheated on her with Phaedra.

She thought about what had just transpired outside the hospital. Did she actually come so close to death? Would her friend have actually pulled the trigger if the police hadn't shown up?

Clyde opened his eyes and saw Luca seated next to him. He managed a smile.

"Hey," she spoke. "I see you're awake. How are you feeling?"

"I could be better," he replied faintly.

"Have you been eating?"

"I'm not too hungry."

Luca didn't mention what happened with Phaedra outside the hospital. He probably wouldn't believe her if she told him anyway, knowing how close they were, or used to be. But, then again, he'd caused the rift between them when he decided to have sex with both women.

She knew that coming to visit Clyde in the hospital was putting her life in danger, but it was a risk she was willing to take. Luca wasn't born yesterday though, and after the failed hit on her life by Squirrel, she decided to call in her connections and cash in on her blackmailing schemes by contacting Judge Holland Lemansky and the local precinct. She gave them the names of all potential threats, from Squirrel down. She would survive by any means necessary.

Her IQ was a weapon of mass destruction. A few of her enemies were destroyed for the reason that, while they were playing checkers, she was playing chess.

Although she gave up Squirrel, World, and, at the last minute, Phaedra, never in her wildest thought did she think when she turned around she would be facing her best friend. It was definitely a hard pill to swallow.

Some might call it snitching, but Luca looked at it as having the drop on everyone. She had the attitude that it was either her or them.

Luca's phone call led to undercover officers staking out the place for days. They had everything they needed— Phaedra's description along with the vehicle she could be driving. And her information was on the money. With Phaedra locked up, that was one down and two to go. Luca didn't have time to feel any sympathy for her former friend. She didn't have time to do anything but survive and build her empire again. She had lost too many people and too much money.

The hospital room felt basic and functional. There were faded walls with streaks where it had been cleaned, and the cold tiled floors looked clean. While there was plenty of room to move about, there was nowhere to get comfortable.

"You need to eat," Luca said to him.

Clyde didn't say anything. He only looked off into the distance.

He didn't look like the sovereign he was anymore. Paralyzed from the waist down, he looked like a withered man dying with cancer. His extreme weight loss made his face sink in, and his eyes looked bigger.

Luca believed he would get better. Maybe one day walk again.

"It's snowing outside," she said, trying to turn his silence into conversation.

"I don't care for the snow right now, Luca," he replied.

"What do you care for right now?"

"To leave here and be myself again," he said, some sarcasm in his tone.

Luca felt she walked into that one. The smile he had when he'd opened his eyes to see her at his bedside seemed long gone. Now someone different was in the room.

She looked out the window from her chair. The blinds were open, showing the bright snowfall outside.

Clyde was turned away from the view, not caring to see the snowfall.

She wanted to say it would get better, but she couldn't predict the future. She didn't see miracles happen in her world. It was always pain and sorrow. It could have been her lying there fucked up and looking crazy.

Would he blame me? Luca thought. Squirrel meant to shoot her, not him. Clyde was just being a hero, and it had cost him his legs. *Would he become a foe in my life also?*

"Next time I come, I'll bring you some food from the outside."

Once again, Clyde didn't respond.

"You're strong, baby. You'll get through this. I know you will. And I'll be there for you. From the stories you told me about your childhood and the trials and tribulations you endured, you will walk away from this hell too."

Clyde took a deep breath. "I know."

Luca smiled. "You will."

Luca decided to turn on the television for them to watch. She spent the entire day with him. When he needed something, she didn't hesitate to get it for him or help change his colostomy bag or wipe him down. She became his private nurse. She tried to bring some humor and conversation into the room, but it started to feel forced.

Clyde was in and out of it. He would sleep mostly, and when he was awake, he just wasn't himself. Even though it was understandable that he was going through a lot, it still felt unreal.

When she looked out the window, the streets were covered with snow, making it look like a winter wonderland. Her car was going to be submerged in it. It was agonizing to think about walking and traveling in the blizzard with her fashionable boots, so she decided to stay the night with him and make herself comfortable in the room, the mountain of snow outside holding her captive.

Luca paid off the head nurse for permission to stay overnight and then nestled herself into the tight, restricted visiting chair and tried to make herself at home. She folded herself into a comfortable position and gazed up at the mounted TV on the wall. The evening news was showing, the sound on low.

Clyde was sleeping again. The nurses regularly entered the room to check on his vitals, and the orderlies came and went, performing their non-medical duties in the room.

There was a weather advisory broadcasting. A significant winter storm was occurring and was becoming an inconvenience to everyone. The highway and roads were becoming unsafe. With six to eight inches of snow expected, it seemed like no one was going home anytime soon. Businesses were closing early, and outside was starting to look like a ghost town.

Luca stood out of her chair and went to the window. She gazed outside, watching city blocks become completely engulfed with whiteness, and traffic on the streets slowing down to a crawl. She couldn't see her own car from the window.

The storm was chaotic but beautiful at the same time.

The weather seemed to mirror her life. She was in a storm herself. She was a falling beauty, highly intelligent, great to look at, but also a woman who caused havoc on so many people's lives, changing the scenery in the drug game and on the streets, like the blizzard outside.

She lingered by the window for a long moment, thinking about how this life would end for her.

The snow had taken over for a moment. It had everyone's attention as it conquered the whole city.

Eventually, though, it was going to melt and disappear and be forgotten until the next snowfall.

Luca didn't want to melt or be forgotten. She didn't want to just disappear like melting snow. She needed to rebuild. She also needed an exit plan from the hostile world she was thrust into not long ago. Having become the dominant bitch in the drug game, she had to be smart enough to know that, sooner or later, everything comes to an end. Even life itself.

Chapter 2

The raunchy lyrics to "Diced Pineapples" blared throughout Crazy Legs, the seedy strip club in Newark, New Jersey. The place was swollen with people, mostly the city's locals, thugs, and drug dealers trying to enjoy themselves. Over a dozen half-naked strippers strutted around the dimly lit club trying to make their money and entice the men ogling at their bodies. It was Sodom and Gomorrah behind the walls of Crazy Legs.

On stage, an endowed chocolate-coated stripper with balloon tits and a sultry look worked the long pole centered in the middle of the stage. Wearing only a pink G-string that her phat ass swallowed up, she twirled around the pole like a gymnast, showing off her flexibility and strength. She was beautiful with her smoky eyes, glossy lips, long, dark hair, and thick, dark eyebrows. Both her arms and the small of her back were swathed with tattoos, and she danced in her stilettos like she was wearing sneakers.

Watching her from across the floor and sitting alone and in silence was World. He sat in the darkest area, almost consumed by the shadows in the corner. He was unapproachable from everything happening, his eyes transfixed on some pussy.

A little tipsy, World took a sip from his beer and slouched in his seat. Wearing all black, he had a concealed 9 mm in his waistband. He got the gun through security by passing the tall, beefy bouncer at the door five hundred dollars to ignore the weapon. World refused to go anywhere and not carry his gun. He was a marked man with enemies coming at him from every direction.

With the stroke of his sword, he'd taken over almost all of Harlem, Brooklyn, and Queens, with Bad Boy selling like Beyoncé tickets. But it all came with a cost. He lost plenty of good soldiers along the way, and he was losing more of his sanity—what little that he had left anyway. Doc's death still weighed heavily on his heart. He missed his friend. He missed their capers.

World took a swig from his beer, his eyes set on the stripper. He was in somewhat of a trance, thinking about his next step. He needed to assemble a new group of lunatics who didn't give a fuck about anything. They had to act and think like him. They had to be so crazy that the streets would tremble in fear when they came around. Even the most hardcore gangster would tread lightly when around his crew. He had enough money to buy anyone, even their souls.

World knew that enemies could even be the ones closest to you. Luca was an example of that. He still burned inside to have her destroyed some way, to taunt and humiliate her. But he felt that there was a bigger threat looming his way.

He may have been crazy, but he wasn't a fool. He knew that sooner or later Xavier and his corrupt merry men of officers were going to be a problem. They'd helped him rise, and they'd made tons of money together, but lately they had been displeased with his actions. The minute they saw him as a problem, it would be easier to kill him than keep him around. He wasn't going to rest until he thought of a way to destroy them before the inevitable came marching his way.

The club was almost bursting at its seams because so many men were inside having a good time, turning up, and politicking. World needed to free his mind from his tribulations.

The chocolate beauty on stage worked her sweet magic, getting butt naked in front of the crowd, spreading her legs, playing with her tits, and shaking her ass and making it clap to the beat. The stage was raining money.

For a moment, she locked eyes with World and smiled.

After her mind-blowing segment, she collected her tips and picked up her clothing. She walked off the stage a paid bitch. Her attention was on World for some reason.

World stayed seated with his eyes on her, drinking his beer and looking like the world was his.

She approached him with an engaging smile and asked, "You gonna sit and watch pussy all day?"

"I can do whatever the fuck I want," he replied.

"Including do me too," she returned. "You need some company?"

World motioned his hand to the chair opposite of him. She sat, her body glistening with sweat, her black skin looking flawless, her smile revealing teeth white like pearl.

"So, you gonna buy a bitch a drink?" she asked.

"What you drinkin'?"

"Rum and Coke."

World didn't rush to comply with her drink order. He didn't need to rush for anyone, and he didn't need to appease no one. He was a kingpin, but tonight, you would never know it. He remained low key and nonchalant around her and everyone else. He didn't flash any heavy jewelry, nor was he dressed down to the nines like he usually was. He was simple in a black coat, a plain T-shirt underneath, black jeans, black ski-hat, and black Timberlands. In fact, he was dressed like he was about to pull a caper.

But what he did have in his pockets was money, and lots of it. Five thousand dollars cash rolled up into three separate rubber bands. He pulled out a few hundred-dollar bills, and the dancer was impressed.

"Damn," she uttered, her eyes widening.

He removed two hundred-dollar bills from his wad and dangled it in front of her. "What's ya name?" he asked.

"Desire."

He smiled. "Listen, Desire, I got two hundred for you if you do a simple favor for me."

"Honey, we can make it as simple as you want." She smiled widely and moved her chair closer to him.

World remained stoic. "I don't need sex," he said.

"So what you need? You on that freaky shit, then that's gonna cost you more money, honey."

"Nah, no freaky shit, just a favor, and the two hundred is yours."

"So what's the favor?"

World looked over by the bar. He fixed his eyes on a young thug clad in a gray velour sweat suit seated at the end of the bar, nursing a beer and drooling over a Spanish chick. He looked back at Desire and said, "I want you to get ya drink and then seduce the nigga with the blue Yankee cap and gray sweat suit at the bar. Take him somewhere and treat him really nice."

"That's it, you paying for another nigga's pleasure?"

"Something like that."

Desire found it strange, but for two hundred dollars, she wasn't about to question why.

World passed her the first hundred-dollar bill.

"You want me to go over there naked or dressed?"

"However you please. Just get his attention. Have him leave somewhere wit' you, make your money, and do what you do best. And whatever you do, don't mention I sent you."

Desire nodded. "Baby, the way I look, I can lead a fish out of water and have it thinking it will live forever." She walked over and didn't look back at World.

World sat coolly, smoking a cigarette and watching Desire perform her job. She situated herself next to the man by the bar and easily started a conversation with her mark. They started talking. The man smiled. He bought her a drink, and they had each other's undivided attention.

It took her only fifteen minutes to have him leave the bar and go somewhere privately with her. When they both stood up, World stood up too. He left a twenty-dollar tip on the table and keenly watched both of their actions.

Desire walked back his way.

World hid in the shadows like some demonic figure, and when she was near, he pulled her to the side and asked, "Where's he taking you?"

"To his car. I'm gonna get dressed. Where's the rest of my money?"

World gave her the second hundred.

Desire smiled. "With the hundred he's paying me for a good time and plus your two hundred, y'all making this a wonderful night for me."

The money meant nothing to World. There was plenty where that came from. She was excited over peanuts, when he was harvesting the entire farm. He didn't trust her, but she was the solution to his minor problem. He allowed her to walk into the dressing room to change into her street clothes.

The man she was leaving with was waiting patiently by the bar. He was of average height with dark, short hair and a lean build. He looked like a simpleton, but he wasn't.

World was smart enough to know that he hadn't come alone. He had goons situated throughout the club, watching his back. The dude was young, in his late teens, and the son to one of World's enemies, a man named Big Show.

Lately, World and Big Show had been at odds with each other. Big Show was supposed to be the new kid on the block, or the old hustler who'd just come home from doing a lengthy bid and trying to make some noise again. He was an OG with a cocky attitude. He still had clout, still felt he was lethal in the game, and thought retirement was for fools. Harlem supposedly was still his grounds, and he didn't get the memo that life goes on after incarceration.

Big Show started creating problems for World, like pushing his hustlers off the corners, taxing drug dealers in the area, and kidnapping one of World's female workers and beating her like she was a dude. Big Show had been calling World out and challenging him like he was some fuck boy.

Big Show was definitely a problem, and World was ready to fix it. He needed to send out a message to the man that he was nobody to fuck with.

It wasn't a secret that Big Show's son, Jerome, was a pussy-craved nigga who was trying to fuck everything moving. He frequented the strip clubs from New York to New Jersey, but his favorite was Crazy Legs.

World knew Jerome's pedigree. He'd stalked him for a few days and decided to use him to relay a message back to Big Show. It was going to be a strong and clear message with no hazy meanings.

Desire exited the dressing room in her jeans, white sneakers, winter coat, and a ball cap pulled over her eyes. She went from erotic to plain Jane effortlessly. She walked by World without any acknowledgement and headed back to Jerome, who smiled seeing her coming his way. They spoke briefly, and then she followed him out the door.

Like World expected, an ugly, tall goon followed them. He was protection for Big Show's only son.

World trailed behind all of them, keeping his head low.

Crazy Legs was in a gang-infested area, and leaving the club alone could be a high risk. It was known for shootouts, fights, robberies, and murders. But none of that concerned World. He kept his pistol close and slyly followed behind Jerome, Desire, and the tall man.

They climbed into an Aston Martin DB9 Volante parked down the street from the club. The convertible was fully loaded with red leather seats and a high-tech dashboard. Desire was ecstatic when she got inside. It was her first time in an exotic car.

The tall man walked to the driver's side. Jerome rolled down the window.

World watched from a short distance, remaining unseen. It seemed like the tall man was advising Jerome about something.

Jerome nodded. He then said, "I'll be parked around the block."

The tall man nodded his head.

The car started, and the engine roared like thunder. It was a powerful car, not just for show, but it was built for speed too. Desire was electrified. She planned on doing him so right that when she was done, he would throw all his money at her.

Before Jerome could pull out of his parking spot, she was nuzzled against him, fondling his crotch, kissing his neck.

World watched the Aston Martin turn the corner. He knew they weren't going too far away from his security. He had an idea where they would be parked. His speculation was confirmed when he observed the tall man trek to the end of the block and post up there, every so often looking around as he waited.

The industrial area was bare of traffic and people during the night, except for the many parked cars on the block because of the strip club. The stickup kids loved the area because of the lack of police patrols and the many closed business. It was a haven for crime and punishment.

Around the corner was a dark and secluded alleyway that led to a dead end. It was the perfect spot for sex with just one way in and one way out. The only witnesses around were the rats scurrying about.

World went to his car, got the silencer, and twisted it onto the tip of his barrel. He didn't need any unwanted attention. It would be quick and clean. He hid the pistol behind him as he walked toward the tall man pretending to be some local drunk wandering about. When he got closer, the tall man looked his way, scowling. He kept his eyes on World and looked at him with great suspicion.

"Yo, cross the street," the tall man told him. "There isn't shit this way for you."

"C'mon, man," World said, "I'm just walkin'. Yo, you got a dollar, nigga?"

"I ain't got shit for you but trouble if you come any closer," the tall man stated gruffly.

"Trouble?" World laughed. He was already looking for trouble. He wasn't about to turn away from a fight. He had great plans for Jerome, and no one was going to stop him.

The tall man kept his hand near his concealed pistol, his eyes on the strange man appearing out of the blue.

World continued walking the tall man's way, defying his commands. He gripped the 9 mm tightly, hiding it from his view and staggering like he was walking on a seesaw.

"Yo muthafucka, you deaf?" The tall man stormed World's way, reaching for his weapon with the intent to pistol-whip World and show him a violent lesson.

"Nah, I ain't deaf. I just don't give a fuck."

Suddenly, World sprung the gun from around his back and aimed. The tall man tried to counter, but he was a few seconds too late. The silencer muffled the sound of gunfire as two bullets ripped through his chest, and he collapsed against the pavement.

World hurried to the body and hid it between two parked cars. He looked around to make sure it was all clear. He smiled. Now it was time to have some fun. He went toward the dead end alleyway and could see the car parked in the dark. It was time to send that message to Big Show now.

With his pants around his ankles, his legs spread slightly, and his dick deep in Desire's mouth, Jerome moaned as Desire's head bobbed up and down in his lap. Her mouth wide open, she wrapped her lips around his hard dick and took him deeply into her mouth. She slid her mouth up and down on him a few times.

"Ooooh! Ooooh! Shit! Oh shit! Damn! Ugh! Ooooh!" Jerome cooed. "Damn! Your mouth feels so good." His breathing was ragged as he reclined in his seat and groaned loudly from the sensation.

Desire continued to suck his dick and jerk him off simultaneously.

"Oh shit! Oh fuck! Damn, girl, it feels so fuckin' good. Suck that big dick. Ooooh, you gonna make me fuckin' come! Oh shit!"

Suddenly, their sexual rendezvous was interrupted when shards of glass landed all over the two of them. Desire was so startled by the sound, she accidentally sank her teeth into Jerome's flesh, crunching down on his dick.

He screamed out in agony. "Aaaaaaaaaaaaaaaaahhhh!"

Before the two of them could sense what was going on, World was all over them.

Jerome was hunched over, gripping his dick and screaming in pain, blood on his hand. She had almost bitten his dick off.

Desire was shocked to see World aiming his gun at her. She was so dumbfounded, she said, "I'll give you back your two hundred."

"Keep it," World told her. He fired two bullets into her face, and she slumped over the dashboard, her blood decorating the front seat.

31

Jerome was still in pain. World didn't care for his hollering. He started to pistol-whip him before snatching him out of the driver's seat.

Jerome landed on his side with his pants still around his ankles and his dick still bleeding.

World aimed the gun at his head, but killing him right away was too easy. He had better plans for the son of the man who was trying to reclaim Harlem. World gagged Jerome, bound his limbs, and threw him into the trunk. He tossed the stripper's body to the side, leaving it with the trash, and took off in the expensive car.

***

Big Show woke up in his king-size bed in his West Side apartment with the morning sun percolating through the windows. He yawned and was about to start his day. He noticed that the young beauty he came home with the night before wasn't in the bed with him. She was a freak—a feisty Dominican with big tits and some good pussy. She did things to Big Show he would never forget. He was naked underneath the sheets, his dick still recuperating from her tight, wet pussy.

When he rose up from his lying position, he was surprised to see a black garbage bag at the foot of his bed. It sat there like a gift left for him. It appeared something was inside of it.

He carefully got out of bed and looked around. The woman who had sexed him down seemed long gone, like she'd had disappeared into the night. He was naked, his belly hanging over his dick, and the hair on his chest stood up. He knew something was wrong.

He collected his gun from the drawer beside his bed and cautiously approached the strange black bag that someone had left. *Did she leave it there?*

He slowly picked up the bag. It was to some extent lightweight, something small inside. With his gun in one hand and the bag in the other, he carefully emptied out the bag, and when the contents landed on the bed, Big Show jumped back like he had been hit with electricity.

"What the fuck!" he screamed like a madman.

Jerome's bloody severed head spilled out of the trash bag. His dead eyes looked up at his father in an excruciating stupor, along with his open mouth in fright. Carved on the forehead were the bloody words "Leave now!"

Big Show was grief-stricken. He couldn't believe what he was seeing. Someone had the boldness to brutally murder his only child. He fell to his knees in tears. "What monster!" he cried out. "What fuckin' monster would do this?"

He released his grip from the .45 he was clutching. He closed his eyes tightly and lowered his head. It was hard for him to imagine the horror his son went through for his father's sins.

Big Show had no idea the evil he was up against when dealing with World, who was a first-class lunatic. They said he didn't have a soul, that he was the devil's son, and that he got his name World because he went against the world like a king without an army and was conquering kingdoms.

Chapter 3

Luca decided to trade in her pearl-white Benz for something less conspicuous. Everyone knew it was her car, and the Benz attracted too much attention. She had decided to move back in with her grandmother, and with several dangerous muthafuckas yearning to see her demise, she had to play it smart. And riding around in an expensive car was not playing it smart.

She traded in her Benz for a station wagon, a white Subaru Outback. The dealer thought she was insane, but she knew she still had the Audi S8 parked in Rockaway Park.

Luca was staying with her grandmother so she could be closer to Clyde. She had tried staying with Lucia, but on the second day she knew it wasn't going to work out. Her mother was just too nosy. Lucia constantly came with too many questions, lectures, and parables. Luca wanted peace, and she needed to think. Wanting to remap her life and do things differently, she was in no mood for an interrogation from her mother.

After Clyde was shot, she drove to Rockaway Park, grabbed a few things and hid out from Squirrel and World in plain sight—back in her Brownsville neighborhood in her grandmother's cramped apartment. Her Rockaway Park home created too many problems for her, and left bad memories.

First, there was Detective Charter viciously assaulting her and nearly beating her to death. She could still feel his hands gripping her fragile neck. Second, World was repeatedly breaking into her place and taunting her. She still had no idea how he was going in and out without a trace. Squirrel knew about her location too. Her home in Rockaway Park was more of a minefield than a home— shit just kept on happening there.

The only valuables she left there were her kilos of drugs and her money. She hated to leave them there, but she had nowhere to stash them. She figured it would be too risky to move it with the whirlwind of chaos surrounding her. The first chance she got, she was going to place it all into private storage.

Feeling everything was in a secure location, Luca didn't dwell on losing her product again. Besides, what were the odds of her making the same mistake twice? Everyone who knew about the hidden safe was dead.

Luca placed the .380 into her coat pocket, climbed out of her Subaru Outback, and walked to the project building. The snow was melting. Two days after the crippling blizzard swept over the city and shut everything down from Long Island to New Jersey, city streets were still being plowed, mountains of plowed snow coated the side streets and the sidewalks, parking was a nightmare, and people were still digging their cars out.

Clothed in layers of winter clothing and her boots, she moved like her old self again, walking quietly with her head down, the blue wig absent from her head and her jewelry stashed in a safe place. She wanted to keep a low profile, knowing Squirrel and World were still out there. Phaedra was locked up, so that was one less concern for her.

Luca walked into the lobby and took the polluted concrete stairs to her grandmother's apartment, since the elevator was out of order.

It was early afternoon, and everyone seemed to have stayed home because of the snow. Music blared from various apartments, the strong scent of weed permeated the air, and a teen mother could be heard yelling at her kids. The narrow hallway with graffiti all along its walls felt like it was getting smaller and smaller as Luca walked toward the apartment.

Luca had just spent the morning with Clyde, who was healing rapidly but still paralyzed from the waist down. She wanted to take a shower, a quick nap, and then head back to the hospital to be with him. Mostly, her time went to helping him rehabilitate.

Luca's grandmother gave her a key so she wouldn't be disturbing her by ringing her bell or knocking on the door whenever she showed up. She walked inside, and the place was quiet. Too quiet. Lucinda always had some gospel playing or was cooking. And her grandmother wasn't in her usual spot—seated in the kitchen gazing out the window and being the neighborhood watch.

The apartment was cluttered with her grandmother's things, and it was hard for Luca to get used to the strange smell of Bengay. Her grandmother was a wonderful woman, but it was definitely hard living with her.

"Grandma, I'm home," she called out.

There was no answer.

"Grandma, where are you?"

When her grandma didn't answer a second time, Luca became worried. Lucinda was an old woman with health risks, and the last thing Luca needed was another loved one in the hospital.

Luca quickly went to her grandmother's bedroom and pushed open the door. She sighed with relief when she saw her grandmother sleeping in her bed with a *People* magazine next to her. The old woman had read herself to sleep.

Luca managed to smile. The five-foot-five elderly woman with her frail body and thinning gray hair was still as tough as a pit bull. She may have been small with multiple health issues, but Grandma Lucinda was still a vivacious woman who didn't take shit from anyone. She was a Christian woman, but she was also an opinionated and dogmatic woman.

Luca gazed at her sleeping grandma for a minute. She thought about so many things. Her grandma was always advising her, telling her stories from the time she grew up. She loved her grandma dearly, so it was a horror in Luca's mind to think about her dying. Whenever she needed a place to stay, Lucinda took her in. Whenever she needed someone to talk to because her own mother was incarcerated or running the streets, Lucinda was there. Even when she became a drug queenpin and the gossip about her spread through Brooklyn like an STD, Lucinda always believed there was hope for her granddaughter; that she would better her life.

She walked into her grandmother's room and covered her with the sheet. Inside the bedroom were so many memories from her grandmother's past—awards for past achievements, framed photos from her younger years as a teenager growing up in South Carolina, and pictures of her husband, Luca's grandfather, a very handsome, distinguished-looking man. He was an ex-Marine, a sergeant, and had fought in the Korean War and in Vietnam. He was educated and ambitious. There were many photos of the two of them together, and you could tell that they were both profoundly in love. They had been married for over thirty years until his passing when Luca was just an infant.

Luca decided to linger in her grandmother's room for a moment. She was rarely in the old woman's bedroom, but it was somewhat fascinating to see her family's history. It felt like she had traveled back in time looking at old photos of the neighborhood and old news clippings about her grandfather's bravery and accomplishments from the wars he'd fought in.

Luca had only heard stories about how he took on drug dealers with his protesting and personal war on drugs.

Coming home from Vietnam, he was infuriated by the heroin that flooded his neighborhood and seeing some of his fellow soldiers strung out on drugs. He decided to do something about it and went against the drug dealers in the ghetto, putting his own life at risk. Luca's grandfather was determined to better his community. He was quoted in one article, saying, "It's a shame to fight for your country and then come home and see your country not fighting for our equality."

Luca read several articles about her grandfather. She wished she had known him, but would he want to know her right now? She had become a drug dealer and murderer. The core of her soul was acid. She'd tainted her family's name and followed in her mother's footsteps. He would be spinning in his grave if he knew what his daughter and granddaughter had become.

Being in her grandmother's room, her emotions started to run on high. She placed her grandfather's picture back on the shelf and quickly left the room. Guilt started to swallow her up. What made her walk inside there and leave so suddenly? Was it the spirit of her grandfather? Whatever it was, she felt this sudden force around her. The tears trickled down her face like a river.

Luca closed her grandmother's door and retreated to her own bedroom. She closed the door and sat at the foot of her bed. She dried away her tears and tried to pull herself together.

Luca spent an hour just sitting on her bed, thinking. The quietness around her was comforting, and being in her grandmother's apartment made her feel somewhat secure. It was a place where she could sleep without disturbance, and where she felt loved and respected all the time.

Luca undressed and went into the bathroom. She filled the tub with soothing, warm water and submerged herself neck deep into the water. The lights were off, and the bathroom door was ajar. She exhaled and closed her eyes.

While enjoying the bathtub, she thought about the choices she had made and the people who had come in and out of her life, either by her hands or not.

She also couldn't stop thinking about Clyde. Every minute, every hour, he was on her mind. She was in love with him. They matched wits, and they'd both come from troubled homes growing up. Clyde understood her completely. She felt like herself around him. Everything that Squirrel wasn't, he was.

But images of her man fucking Phaedra would abruptly flow into her head and she would clench her fist tightly with the urge to punch something. Just thinking about Clyde sticking his dick into what used to be her best friend nearly made her go insane. But she forgave him, right? He'd saved her life when Phaedra tried to take it.

Luca submerged herself under water, holding her breath, not wanting to come up anytime soon. Once again, she wanted to close her eyes and be somewhere else. Thirty seconds went by, and she was still holding her breath under water. She thought about her next move—it was going to be with Clyde.

Fifty seconds went by. Still under water, she thought

about Squirrel and how foolish she was to ever think he'd actually loved her and would leave his baby mama for her. Seventy seconds went by, and she thought about the people who betrayed her and why? She thought about what she had left in life—her money and her drugs stashed in Rockaway Park. Ninety seconds went by, and she felt like she couldn't breathe at all. She fought to keep herself submerged.

Luca kept fighting, trying to not breathe. It was difficult. *Why is it always so fuckin' difficult?* she screamed inside her head. She couldn't hold on any longer. She needed to breathe. She felt herself blacking out.

She thrust herself out of the water and took in a gulp of air and inhaled intensely. She felt winded and puffed out. She felt like she'd run a mile because she was breathing so hard. She lingered in the tub and continued thinking. She didn't want to feel like she was drowning anymore. So who was submerging her?

***

Luca treated Clyde to lunch in his private hospital room. She'd brought Asian cuisine from Nobu. She knew her man was tired of eating the bland, tasteless hospital food.

Luca massaged Clyde's body as they talked, even laughed a bit, while dining on ginger lobster, oysters, and shrimp fried rice. Every day he seemed to be getting better and better. The doctors told him he could start physical therapy soon, but his chances of ever walking again were slim to none.

After dinner, Luca noticed Clyde's sudden mood change and figured it was the medication he was taking. "What's wrong?" she asked.

Clyde gazed at her, uncertainty in his eyes. He heaved a sigh. "I don't know where to start."

"Just talk to me." Luca took his hand into hers and smiled. She felt she could deal with whatever he needed to tell her.

"I don't think I can do this anymore," he said.

Luca was taken aback. "What?"

"This thing with us—"

"What about us?" Luca let go of his hand, fearing the worst was about to come out of his mouth. She didn't know what he was trying to say, but her gut told her it was going to be frightful news.

"I've been lying to myself for too long about us."

"Just say it, Clyde," she spat.

"I'm in love with Phaedra."

Luca sat there, shocked at what he'd just confessed. Did she hear him right? How and why? She felt faint suddenly. This couldn't be happening to her, not again.

"What?"

"It's something I can't explain."

"Fuckin' explain it." Her eyes were brimming with anger and sadness.

"It's complicated," he said faintly.

"Complicated?"

Luca wanted to scream. She wanted to attack him. She felt the sting of rejection again, and it was always an unbearable feeling. When Luca saw Phaedra run out of Clyde's apartment half-dressed after the shooting, visions of Nate and Naomi flashed before her eyes like a bad movie.

Briefly, she'd wanted both Clyde and Phaedra dead, but when she realized Clyde was willing to die for her, she felt it was truly love. When he woke up out of his coma and the first thing he did was call out her name, it was solidified. She told herself that she would actually forgive him as well as Phaedra for their betrayal, something she was unable to do in the past. She wanted to do it because she truly loved them both.

But now, after hearing the grim news, she wanted to see both of them dead—brutally murdered and placed into the cold ground.

Luca yelled, "How the fuck is it complicated?" She fought hard to hold back her tears, but her voice cracked under the emotions she was going through.

"There's a lot going on with you . . . with me, with us."

"I'm by your bedside night and day taking care of you, loving you, and you do this shit to me?"

"Luca, I'm sorry."

"Fuck your apologies, you piece of shit!" she screamed. "Fuck you!"

Luca's rant echoed out into the hospital hallway, giving the hospital staff reason to enter the room.

"Is everything okay in here?" the day nurse asked.

Clyde answered, "Yes, we're fine, nurse."

The nurse looked at Luca, standing over Clyde's bed, her back turned to the nurse. "Ma'am, are you okay?"

"I'm fuckin' fine."

"Well, I'm going to have to ask that you leave if you keep up this disturbance."

"I was fuckin' leaving anyway."

"I don't want to have to call security up here," the nurse said with matching attitude. "Visiting hours been over, and he needs his rest. You need to leave."

Luca was seething inside. She felt the urge to spin around and assault the condescending bitch.

"This is your only warning." The nurse turned around on her white crocs and exited the room, leaving Luca standing there with egg on her face.

"Luca—"

"Don't. Just don't."

Luca took a deep breath and calmed herself down, but she couldn't help wondering if Clyde had influenced Phaedra into trying to kill her. It was a far-fetched thought, but in her strange and bizarre world, anything was possible. Once again, visions of Nate fucking Naomi, and Squirrel being with Angel flooded her head. Why was she always not enough for these men?

Luca continued to hold back her tears. She leaned forward and gave Clyde a soft kiss on his lips and then whispered to him, "You're no different than Nate. He thought he could fuck my best friend Naomi and get away with it. He was so wrong. I'm thinking you and Phaedra should do a double date with Nate and Naomi, all of you, living unhappily ever after."

She turned away from him and exited the room.

Chapter 4

The Brooklyn thug named K'wan and his friend Roscoe forced a local drug dealer named Parker at gunpoint up three flights of stairs in the Van Dyke Houses in Brownsville. The midnight hour meant the building didn't have the buzz of residents coming and going.

There was a temporary struggle with their mark in the stairway, with Parker growling, "Fuck y'all muthafuckas!"

But a harsh pistol-whipping made him comply.

"Move, nigga! Hurry the fuck up!" K'wan shouted in his captive's ear with his 9 mm placed to the back of his head, finger on the trigger.

"You fuckin' heard him," Roscoe said. "Fuck around and we gon' blow ya fuckin' brains out!"

K'wan and Roscoe were a deadly duo. But K'wan was a nightmare—ruthless, dangerous, and prone to violent outbursts with severe anger issues. He would kill a person who crossed him quickly with any object that happened to be lying around. Basically, he was a psychotic, murderous thug.

K'wan and Roscoe beat and tortured Parker severely just to have him give up the stash house. His face was a bloody mess, his nose was crooked and broken, and his right eye was swollen shut.

K'wan forced Parker onto the floor in the narrow hallway. He held him closely at gunpoint with the threat of death repeatedly exclaimed into his ear. Parker was a lieutenant for the Supreme team, a fledging drug organization in Brownsville. K'wan was ready to shut them down and take everything they had. This was K'wan and Roscoe's umpteenth risky caper, and each one was paying off, one kicked-down door at a time. He and Roscoe were truly feared in the hood.

It wasn't too long ago that K'wan was the one running shit in the ghetto, becoming one of the biggest drug dealers in Brooklyn with his own fierce crew and stash house to protect from the wolves. His luck suddenly changed when Luca came through with her Bad Girl product and flooded the market with superior product. Then World came through and killed all of his competition with Bad Boy.

At one time, K'wan had raged war on everyone encroaching onto his territory—shootouts ensued, people were murdered. But the hill he was climbing was so steep that, once he lost his footing, death awaited him at the bottom. K'wan was a survivor, and he didn't fear anyone, no matter how fierce their reputation. In his street war with Luca's goons, he took out a few of Luca's soldiers and hated Kool-aid with a passion, until Kool-aid's demise at the hands of a corrupt police officer.

However, once K'wan's drug money started to dry up because of the bloodshed, inferior product, numerous arrests, and an absent connect, he began doing stickups again. It's what he knew best—how to take from other muthafuckas.

K'wan forced Parker to Apartment 3D, the stash house he yearned to rip off. He gripped the back of Parker's torn shirt and thrust the gun into the small of his back. He and Roscoe made sure to keep out of sight from the peephole in the door.

"Knock, muthafucka, or I'll blow ya fuckin' back out," K'wan said.

Parker scowled before knocking.

K'wan was on high alert, watching and waiting. He was carrying twin 9 mms, one digging into Parker's back, the other concealed under the black coat he wore. Roscoe carried a sawed-off shotgun in his hands, and a Glock was tucked in his waistband.

A loud voice came from the other side of the door. "Who?"

"It's me, Parker. Open the fuckin' door."

"A'ight."

They heard locks turning, and the steel door being opened.

Once K'wan saw his window of opportunity, he pushed Parker into the apartment with brute force, knocking him into the man behind the door, and they rushed inside like police serving a warrant. Parker tumbled over his cohort, while K'wan executed his violent stickup.

"Get the fuck down! Get down!" K'wan screamed out, with him and Roscoe sweeping through the room, trying to maintain order and to keep from getting shot.

"Fuck around and get shot tonight!" Roscoe shouted. "Fuck wit' us!"

Three men were caught off guard in the living room.

K'wan held them at gunpoint, while Roscoe hurried through the three-bedroom apartment making sure there weren't any surprises. There was a naked bitch in one of the bedrooms. Roscoe forced her out and made her join everyone in the living room. They made everyone get down on their stomachs, kissing the floor.

"Where the shit at?" K'wan asked.

No one answered.

Roscoe cocked back the shotgun. "Y'all think we fuckin' playin'?" He pointed the sawed-off shotgun at the back of the naked girl's head.

She whimpered and begged for her life.

Someone quickly said, "The shit is in the speakers."

K'wan didn't believe it because music was playing. "You lying, nigga." He stepped to the bitch in a threatening manner, ready to shoot.

The same man shouted, "I'm not fuckin' lying. They in the fuckin' speakers."

K'wan motioned to Roscoe to check it out.

Roscoe carefully inspected the speakers and found out how to remove the woofers. He slowly removed the material and reached inside pulling out several kilos of cocaine and a few bundles of cash. "Bingo!" He smiled like a kid on Christmas Day.

K'wan nodded. "That's what I'm talkin' about."

"You got what you want, let us be," someone exclaimed.

"Yeah, let y'all be. Right. I feel you on that, muthafucka," K'wan said coolly right before he unleashed his fury.

The first shot tore through the man's head, spilling his flesh and blood all over the floor and the people beside him.

When the bitch started screaming, Roscoe quickly shut her up with a shotgun blast to the back of her head. Her skull exploded like a pumpkin falling on a landmine.

They quickly extinguished the other three men execution-style and hurried out of the apartment with the goods.

***

K'wan and Roscoe counted their take in the depths of a shabby apartment building a few blocks from Rockaway Avenue. Money, drugs, and guns were spread out on the table. With a cigarette dangling from his mouth and a bottle of E & J beside him, K'wan nodded to a Jay-Z track and grinned as he counted hundred after hundred.

"Yeah, we came up wit' this hit," K'wan said.

"How much so far?"

"About twenty stacks and, wit' the coke, we talkin' 'bout fifty stacks easy."

Roscoe smiled. "I told you they were holdin' some serious weight up in that spot. Was I wrong, K'wan?"

"Nah, you were on point, Roscoe," K'wan replied nonchalantly.

"My source always be on point."

K'wan threw a dubious gaze at his partner in crime. "Yeah, your source."

K'wan had a personal vendetta on his mind, and he was ready to raise hell on those who had caused his fall from drug boss to petty stickup kid. He was determined to rise back to the top and reclaim what was rightfully his.

He took a pull from the cigarette between his lips and blew out smoke. He placed the ki's back into the garbage bag and divided up the cash.

Roscoe felt proud to be back working capers with his friend again. He'd come home from doing a bullet on Rikers Island and couldn't wait to get back into his treacherous lifestyle.

K'wan handed him $10,000, his portion of the cash.

"Yeah tonight, I'm gonna put this cash to some good use, find me a nice bitch to pop off wit' and ride out. Feel what I'm sayin', my nigga?" Roscoe gleefully leafed through hundred after hundred.

K'wan replied halfheartedly, "Yeah, I feel what you sayin'."

Roscoe placed his cash into two separate pockets of his jacket and turned to make his exit. He gave K'wan dap and was set to have a great time tonight. They planned on stashing the ki's of cocaine somewhere secure and profiting from them later. K'wan had an out-of-state connect that was interested in purchasing them.

"Be safe, my nigga," K'wan said.

"I will."

Roscoe headed for the exit, but before he could take three steps toward the doorway, K'wan immediately picked up his pistol, outstretched his arm, aimed it at the back of Roscoe's head, and fired multiple shots into his skull. Roscoe dropped dead by his feet, his blooding spilling out of his head.

"Snitch muthafucka!" K'wan glared down at the body. He crouched over the body, went through his pockets, and removed the cash.

Roscoe used to be a friend, but word had gotten out that he had been running his big mouth to keep his freedom. Instead of doing hard time for the drug charge he was hit with, he gave up Dwayne, K'wan's little brother. Roscoe received a lesser sentence from the prosecutor's office, doing only one year on Rikers Island. He didn't think K'wan would ever find out. Because of Roscoe, Dwayne was still on Rikers Island awaiting his trial with a $100,000 bail that couldn't be paid.

K'wan grabbed everything in the basement and immediately left, leaving Roscoe's body there to rot. His former friend deserved to burn in hell for his transgression against his family.

K'wan loved his little brother. Dwayne was the only family he had left. He couldn't afford to pay Dwayne's bail, so robbing and killing was the only way to raise the money.

He walked out the building with a cool conscience, whistling a melody, not even giving a second thought that he'd killed a friend. He walked to his car, tossed the goods into the trunk, and climbed behind the wheel. He had another important engagement he needed to be present for. His girl had called him and said she had some important news to tell him, and plus, he was horny.

He lingered behind the wheel of his Maxima for a moment looking pensive. The block was quiet, the cold freezing his windows. He lit another cigarette and smoked for a moment, Dwayne on his mind. He knew his brother could handle himself in jail, but the thought of him getting heavy time because of Roscoe's betrayal haunted him.

Dwayne was only nineteen, but he was already a force to be reckoned with, becoming a lethal young nigga having the streets on lockdown just like his older brother. Dwayne was moving serious weight, and, like K'wan, he was a beast in Brooklyn.

The state prosecutor had unsealed a 15-count indictment, charging Dwayne with continuing of a criminal enterprise and conspiracy to distribute kilos of cocaine, racketeering conspiracy, extortion, and kidnapping. The indictment was based on the cooperation of Roscoe Clinton, who had already pled guilty to drug possession and grand theft.

A year earlier, K'wan would have been able to pay the high bail, but now things had changed drastically. He started the ignition and drove off, leaving behind the stench of disloyalty and a body to freeze and be chewed on by rats in the concrete basement.

If Roscoe told on Dwayne so easily, K'wan couldn't help but to worry what else the big-mouth snitch talked about to the police and prosecutors. K'wan had committed several murders with Roscoe present. A few murders he did were to help Roscoe out.

There was the time when they were seventeen. Roscoe was pumping crack on his corner that evening when a rival approached him and assaulted him for working their territory. K'wan convinced Roscoe to go back out and work that same corner, despite what the nigga had threatened. K'wan reassured him that he had his back. Roscoe trusted his word and worked the same corner the next day. When the same rival returned looking for a confrontation, K'wan stepped out of the cut and shot the man in the head with everything he had in the clip and walked away with the gun smoking.

It angered K'wan that he didn't see Roscoe's weakness from the beginning. He would have handled him earlier, and his brother wouldn't have been in his predicament.

K'wan drove to Bushwick and parked in front of a two-story flat and got out. He walked toward the structure with his pistol tucked snugly in his waistband and rang the bell. As he waited, he quickly observed his surroundings, knowing he was a man with a list of enemies.

The front door opened, and a curvy, voluptuous woman appeared in front of K'wan. She was wearing a red silk robe and was all smiles.

"Hey, baby." She threw her arms around him and invited him inside.

As K'wan walked into her home, she was all over him with kisses to his neck and lips and ready to jump into his arms. She felt the cold steel protruding from his waistband. It turned her on that her man was a vicious gangster and killer. When they fucked, sometimes he would rub the barrel of a 9 mm against her naked nipples, or massage her clit with the tip of his .38.

"I got some really good news for you, baby," she said.

"What you got for me, Paquitta?"

"You love me?"

"Yeah, you know I do," K'wan replied, wrapping his arms around her curvy waist and squeezing her lovingly.

They passionately locked lips in the foyer. K'wan lifted the back of her robe and clutched her naked booty. Paquitta had ass for days. He loved her body—her shaved pussy, dark nipples, thick thighs, and that ghetto attitude.

He fondled her body and cupped her tits, ready to unzip his jeans and please himself with some of that ghetto loving.

Paquitta untied her robe, revealing her appealing body and teasingly took a few steps back away from him. She was beautifully drunk off his thug loving and murderous smile.

K'wan followed her deeper into the living room. He removed the pistol from his waistband and placed it on the coffee table. He undid his jeans, took off his coat, and pulled his shirt over his head, exposing his chiseled, tattooed body and street wounds.

"What you got to tell me?" he asked.

Paquitta dropped her robe, letting it mesh around her feet and was completely naked for his taking. "C'mere, sexy," she said, gesturing with two fingers.

K'wan stepped toward her, smiling broadly.

Within a span of twenty-four hours, K'wan had killed numerous people, including his best friend, and it didn't bother him at all.

He entangled himself in her seductiveness, and they fervently locked lips again.

She hurriedly pulled out his thick penis and wrapped her manicured nails around it. As she stroked his dick, she said into his ear, "Your brother is coming home, baby. He made bail."

K'wan pushed away from Paquitta. "What the fuck you talkin' 'bout?"

"I thought you would be happy, baby."

"How the fuck my brother made bail?"

"I looked out for you."

"How? Where the fuck did you get a hundred thousand to post his bail, Paquitta?"

"From a friend."

K'wan looked at her suspiciously. "What fuckin' friend? You fuckin' some other nigga?"

"No!" she exclaimed. "I love you. And, besides, he came to me and was asking about you. He heard about Dwayne and decided to post his bail. He wants to meet you, K'wan. He wants to talk some business wit' you, baby."

"What business?"

"I don't know, but ya name rings out, K'wan, and you know we need the money."

K'wan clenched his jaws along with his fists. He shot a murderous look at Paquitta. He wasn't too thrilled about her being in his business and chatting with some other nigga about his future.

"Just talk to him, baby."

"Who the fuck is this nigga you talkin' about?" he shouted.

"His name is World."

"World?" K'wan repeated, a bizarre expression on his face. He knew that name from somewhere.

"He said he got some work for you if you need it, and he's willing to pay you what you worth. Baby, you ain't gotta be out there doin' these stickups. The nigga is running an empire."

"I was running a fuckin' empire, bitch! You want me to become a fuckin' soldier in some next nigga's crew when I was the fuckin' general of my own shit?"

"He just wants to talk to you, baby, that's all. It can't hurt, right?" Paquitta softly said to him.

K'wan wasn't too excited to meet with the man, but he wasn't stupid. If this man was able to bail his brother out of jail, then K'wan might be able to work with him.

Chapter 5

Luca was devastated by Clyde's rejection. She didn't understand it. What was wrong with her? Why did he choose Phaedra? The thought of it made her want to snap. She wanted to hate everyone.

Leaving the hospital, the pain in her heart was throbbing like she was about to explode. She hurried to her car and sped away, not knowing what direction she wanted to go in. She didn't want to be around anyone. She wanted to disappear for a moment and think, really think.

She found herself driving toward her home in Rockaway Park. During the ride, Luca cried her eyes out. She wished she could drive herself into a different life and become someone new, or turn back the hands of time and correct her mistakes.

The hour drive from Brooklyn to Rockaway Park was a sorrowful one, every mile polluted with distraught memories. The farther she traveled from Brooklyn, the deeper her heart sank, and the more her tears flowed. She had lost so much. The men she loved—Nate, Squirrel, and now Clyde—had all betrayed her and broken her heart. Not to mention friends—Naomi, and now Phaedra. She had no one left that she truly loved, no one but her dying grandmother.

Luca had no idea what or who was waiting for her at the home. It was a dangerous place for her to be alone, but she didn't care.

In was late in the evening when Luca arrived in the quiet suburban area with its prime real estate, manicured green lawns, picket fences, and that *Brady Bunch* way of living. The houses on both sides of the street were spread more than a respectable distance from each other, not cramped and packed on top of each other like the projects in Brooklyn.

She navigated her way through Mayberry, and when she rounded the corner to her street, nothing could prepare her for what she saw next.

Luca stopped the car in front of her home, her mouth open in awe. She couldn't believe her eyes. It couldn't be true. This wasn't happening. She only wanted to wake up from the perpetual nightmare she kept plummeting deeper and deeper into. Her house was gone—like *Wizard of Oz* gone.

"Ohmygod! Ohmygod! Ohmygod!" Her eyes teared up again.

There had to be some kind of explanation. Her home couldn't just get up and walk away. She jumped out of her car in disbelief and hurried to what was left—nothing. *What the fuck happened?*

There was nothing left of her home, not even rubble, no indication that a house had even been built there. It left only an unpleasant view in the plush area.

Luca walked all around her property and looked around. The ground beneath her feet felt soft and unsteady. Maybe she was getting dizzy. She stood in an empty quarter where her living room used to be. Then she walked over to where her secret room used to be, and it was all gone—the money and the drugs.

"Why was I so fuckin' foolish to leave it in the same place twice?" she screamed out.

She remembered the old saying: fool me once, shame on you, and fool me twice, shame on me. Shame on her. It was a stupid, stupid move. Luca collapsed down on her knees, feeling beaten, overwhelmed, and overcome with anguish. She had lost everything.

Luca noticed the neighbors' lights come on and then someone pulled back their blinds to see outside. She lifted herself off her knees and walked over to the house. She dried her tears and stormed up the porch and knocked loud enough for the entire neighborhood to hear.

She banged loudly and shouted, "I know someone is fuckin' home! Answer the fuckin' door!" She didn't care if they called the cops or not; she wasn't going anywhere.

A minute later, the porch light came on, and the front door opened up, followed by the screen door. Luca glared at Mrs. Shoals, in a green housecoat, her hair in rollers.

"Luca, what is going on?" Mrs. Shoals asked, looking mystified by Luca's presence.

"Don't act like you didn't know I am here, Mrs. Shoals. I saw you looking out your window. I wanna know what the fuck happened to my fuckin' house. Why isn't it there anymore?"

Mrs. Shoals sighed, looked up and down the block and said, "Come inside. I'll tell you what happened."

Luca stepped inside the woman's well-furnished home and stood in the living room. She was livid.

Mr. Shoals came marching down the stairs tying his robe together. "Tina, who was that knocking on the gotdamn door like that? What is wrong with people today? They have no respect."

When he reached the living room and saw Luca standing there, he turned blue in the face. "Oh," he uttered with embarrassment.

Luca glared at him.

Mr. Shoals could only look at Luca. "I'm sorry about your house."

"Fuck a sorry! What happened?" she spewed, impatience in her tone.

"Do you want some tea?" Mrs. Shoals asked.

Luca didn't have time for their formalities. She wanted them to talk. She knew they knew something. There was no way they could live next door and not see how her house just up and vanished out of nowhere. This wasn't David Copperfield, and she didn't believe in magic.

"I just wanna know what happened."

Mrs. Shoals said, "Two weeks ago your house caught fire."

"What?"

"It was a huge blaze."

"It was a damn inferno, woman," Mr. Shoals said, like it was something he had never seen before.

Luca looked at them in disbelief. "My house caught on fire, how?"

Mrs. Shoals told her, "It was a big fire. It got so out of control, the block had to be evacuated. We heard something like an explosion. We didn't know if it was a gas line or something. The fire department couldn't contain the fire, so your house burned down to the ground."

Luca couldn't believe what she was hearing. She took a seat on their couch, feeling her chest tightening and her breath shortening.

"Luca, are you okay?" Mrs. Shoals asked.

"Get the girl some water."

Mrs. Shoals hurried into the kitchen to fetch Luca some water to drink. Her husband stayed with Luca in the living room. She came back into the room and handed Luca a full glass of cold water.

Luca took it and drank half the glass. She had to somehow get around the unpleasant emotion of losing everything. The way Mr. and Mrs. Shoals looked at her, with deep sorrow, she knew there was more to tell.

"For a minute, everyone thought you were inside," Mrs. Shoals said. "They say it was arson."

"Arson?" Luca repeated.

"The fire department ruled it an arson. They went through the entire structure, picking around everything, thinking you were dead inside, but everyone was relieved to know you weren't inside the place." Mr. Shoals added, "The county had a bulldozer come through and knock it completely down, and they cleared away every bit of debris because it was an eyesore."

"I'm shocked you hadn't heard, Luca. The fire was on the news, and people tried reaching you."

Luca couldn't tell them that she had nearly a hundred voice messages that she chose to ignore because her ex-drug dealing boyfriend was nearly murdered by her other drug dealing jump-off.

"My grandmother is really sick, so I was staying with her."

"Oh, I'm so sorry to hear about that," Mrs. Shoals said.

Everything was too much to take in all at once. She tried to breathe. She tried to think.

"Do you have some place to go?" Mr. Shoals asked.

Luca nodded her head. "I do."

"Well, if you need to, you can stay here for the night," Mrs. Shoals said to her. "I'm truly sorry about everything. You're a sweet young girl, and things will pick up."

What the fuck this bitch know about me? Luca thought to herself. When she had moved in, they didn't come over with baskets of food and smiles to welcome her to the neighborhood. They didn't converse with her when their paths crossed coming and going. She only knew their last name because one day the mailman accidentally delivered their mail to her place and she saw the name Shoal on the envelope.

The Shoals were a proud white couple. Luca knew when they saw a young black girl moving in next door to them, they probably said, "There goes the neighborhood."

The offer to spend the night was tempting, but Luca had to decline. It was funny. First they didn't want to answer their door and deal with her, but now they were opening their home to her. *Why? Because of pity. To help a black girl out and soothe their guilt.*

When the incident had happened with Charter, where she nearly lost her life, the neighbors talked about her like a dog, and not one ever came by after she was out of the hospital to check on her, though they knew she lived alone. Rockaway Park was a racist area. Luca didn't feel comfortable being anywhere near her burnt-down home.

She guzzled the last of the water in the glass and handed it back to Mrs. Shoals. She had a funny feeling about something. Her gut instincts told her there was more to be told and maybe they were withholding something else from her. When Mrs. Shoals gave her husband that particular look, like whether they should tell her or not, Luca knew she was right. She stood up. "Tell me what you're thinking."

Mrs. Shoals replied, "It's not our business to tell."

"Like hell it ain't," Luca barked. "My house is burnt down to the ground and y'all wanna hold shit back?"

Mrs. Shoals glanced at her husband, who in return said, "Might as well go on and tell her everything."

"The people you rent the house from, they're being investigated for the arson," Mrs. Shoals informed her.

"What?" Luca was puzzled.

She rented the house from two Jewish brothers. She didn't want any red flags by paying for the house in cash, so she went through a middleman. The Kabakoff brothers seemed legit in Luca's eyes. She did a background check, as they did one on her too, and the paperwork was legit. So what did she miss? It appeared the Kabakoff brothers, the owners of the home, were in some kind of financial trouble. Hence the reason they'd moved out of their home and into an apartment and Luca was covering the mortgage.

Luca knew she couldn't trust them. In her eyes, they were always sneaky. They burned the house down probably to collect insurance money. She was relieved, though, that she wasn't going to be investigated for something she didn't do. She already had enough on her plate and didn't need any more run-ins with the law. She still had a bad taste in her mouth from dealing with the Rockaway Park PD over Charter's death.

Luca had heard enough. "I need to go," she said to the couple.

She walked out of their home without even saying a simple "Thank you." She was pissed off. It felt like she was about to collapse in their living room and needed to get away. It was always one thing after another.

When she stepped outside into the cool air night, she hollered at herself, *What I'm gonna do now?* Her money and drugs were burned to the ground. She wanted to kick herself for being so stupid to think it was safe again to hide her stash in the house. Never in her wildest imagination did she think the house would catch on fire and burn completely down to the ground. Her landlords had no idea that their evil scheme was going to cost them their lives. They'd fucked with the wrong bitch.

She took one long look at the empty lot where her home used to be and knew it was time to move on. There was nothing there for her anymore.

She dried her tears and climbed into her Subaru Outback. She lit a cigarette, took a few pulls while lingering behind in the driver's seat, and decided to drive farther north. She needed to recoup and try and come back stronger.

She came up with the craziest thing to do. It was going to be a long drive where she planned on heading, but she felt it was the right thing to do. She needed to see the man she'd heard about all her life but had never known.

∗∗∗

The drive to Dannemora, New York was an exhausting one. It took Luca six hours to arrive in the small town, and when she finally did, dawn was breaking. She needed to rest. She checked into a roadside motel with its neon sign, cement floors, Ikea furniture, and prevailing minimalist vibe. She got a room on a shoestring budget and crashed the minute she stepped foot inside.

She slept almost all day, so when she finally awoke, it was almost evening again.

Luca changed clothes and decided she would visit her father the following day. Until then, she would make the best of her stay in the primitive-looking town. She was starving and needed a drink or two to pass the time away.

Stepping out of the motel, Luca felt like she was in the middle of nowhere. It was cold, and snow was everywhere. Dannemora was nestled among the Adirondack Mountains. The closest city was Plattsburgh. It was only considered a city because it had a Super Walmart. Dannemora was home to Clinton Correctional Facility, the largest state prison in New York. Most people who lived in the town either worked at the prison, lived inside the prison, or had family who lived inside the prison. The residents considered their town a great place to live with a small population, providing a safe and friendly atmosphere.

Luca felt it was limbo—fuckin' purgatory for someone coming from the big city. The forests, mountains, and lakes surrounding the region provided great scenery, but the dullness of the area was enough to make her cut her own throat.

She found some subpar entertainment at a nearby bar full of rednecks and easygoing locals. She stood out like a sore thumb with her expensive clothing and New York attitude. She wasn't the only minority in the place, but she felt like an alien. Some of the folks didn't look too accepting of her kind. In her mind, she could almost certainly run this town if she chose to. The highest IQ was probably 90, and the police looked like Keystone Cops.

Who would stop her? But was there any money to be made in a small upstate town? It was just a thought.

Luca sat at the bar and guzzled a beer, minding her business.

A local boy attempted to make conversation with her, a white boy of average height, a lean build, narrow face, and a bad haircut. He wore a plaid shirt and dingy blue jeans. All the men seemed to dress the same. His upstate accent was strong.

Luca laughed inwardly, thinking he was the type of person to have appliances in his front yard, or could spit without opening his mouth.

"Where ya from, ma'am?" he asked.

"The city," Luca replied.

"New York City, huh? Never been myself."

He had probably never seen a woman like her—a young lovely, statuesque beauty wearing high-end fashion. He ogled her. He was somewhat cute, but not in a million years was he Luca's type.

"What brings you to Dannemora?"

"Just stopping through."

"Well, welcome. Can I buy you a drink?"

Why not? Luca thought. She ordered another beer.

The selection of liquor behind the bar was thin, and it seemed like everyone else in the place got loaded on beer more than anything else. The female bartender, who was fifty pounds overweight with auburn hair, handed her a Bud Light.

"I'm Lance," he said, extending his hand.

"Luca," she said, shaking his.

Luca found herself rather entertained by him even though his selection of conversation was meager. He had never left Dannemora, never traveled anywhere far, and had a high-school education. The only city he'd seen was Plattsburgh, which still was a small town in Luca's eyes. He talked about his town fondly and what it was like growing up in upstate New York.

Luca needed to get her mind off Clyde and her home, and Lance was a big help.

An hour later, she decided she would do something even crazier—take him back to her motel room. When she gave him the invitation, Lance was more than willing. He paid the bar tab, and they both exited the small bar.

Outside, she jumped into her Subaru Outback, and Lance got into his car. The hood and one door was a different color from the rest of his car. Luca laughed. He followed the short distance behind her back to the roadside motel.

Lance was wide-eyed and smiling at her beautiful nude skin as she was about to straddle him and place his average, pink-looking sausage inside of her.

"Have you ever been with a black woman before?"

"No, ma'am," he answered, like she was some type of authority figure.

He was hard, but no competition to any of her other lovers. He wasn't even in the ballpark. She grabbed his hard-on and placed the head at the entrance of her pussy.

"Ooooh shit," Lance cried out, feeling the sensation of her wet, tight pussy.

She placed her hands against his small hairless chest, her eyes closed, trying to black out anything negative. She just wanted to feel something good before tomorrow came.

It was going to be a tough day for her. She had never met her father. She didn't want to spend the whole night alone thinking about anything off-putting. The white boy thrusting inside of her was a temporary diversion to keep her from thinking about her father being the first man to be absent in her life, to break her heart and never be around, never mind he was doing a life sentence.

"Fuck me!" Luca cried out, grinding her hips against him, feeling his hands grabbing her ass.

Lance started stroking, his eyes rolling back in his head.

Her legs wrapped around him, she cried out, "More. Fuck me more."

He tried to give her more. He reached up and cupped her tits, pinched her nipples and pounded her. He fucked her deep, and slow and hard. Then he built up his pace, fucking her faster and harder, making her moan and groan.

When she slammed her pussy down on his dick, Lance screamed out, "Damn! You feel so good."

Luca made eye contact with him and rode him like a champion.

He continued to play with her nipples as her juices coated him. "I'm coming," he said.

"Don't come yet," she demanded.

Luca needed to get hers. She needed to feel some fuckin' relief. She felt his pink run-of-the-mill dick twisting and thrusting inside of her. She closed her eyes and dug her nails into his chest.

Lance tried his best, fucking her like a wild animal. There was nothing to hold him back. This was fucking like it was meant to be—huffing and puffing, and juicy, squishing sex.

Luca made herself get to the point of no return. She needed to come. She couldn't hold back any longer, and Lance was trying to hold back too, wanting her to release her orgasm.

Lance shouted, "I'm coming! Yes! Yes!" He grabbed her hips and delivered his come heavily, pouring it all into her, the condom acting as a barricade to prevent it from spilling inside of her. He shivered and howled, feeling the essence of a black woman overcome him.

Luca collapsed beside him. She just had the urge to try something different, and an upstate, redneck, small-town white boy was definitely something different.

Lance looked spent. His thin body glistened in sweat. "Whoo-wee!" he hollered with joy. "Now that was mind-blowing."

Luca chuckled.

"You mind if we could do that again?" he asked.

Luca didn't mind. She was looking forward to it. Tomorrow was about to be a difficult and trying day for her.

They rested for a moment, talked, and then Lance was hard again, penetrating her this time in the missionary position. Luca closed her eyes and put herself into a different mindset. As he fucked her, she thought about her father and couldn't shake the feeling of nervousness.

Chapter 6

The beautiful white wall surrounding the prison seemed more like it was protecting a castle than a maximum-security prison. In fact, the wall could give a visitor the feeling that they'd taken a wrong turn. The white wall seemed to stretch for miles, covering acres of land, with guard towers overlooking every inch of it. Just across the street from the intimidating structure stood local shops and long-standing homes and businesses. Formerly the home of rappers Tupac and Shyne, as well as the Son of Sam, Clinton Correctional was the largest and third-oldest maximum-security prison in the state. The prison provided employment for many people in the area.

Luca walked into the prison's visiting room feeling like she was about to make the biggest mistake of her life. Coming to see her father was a spur-of-the-moment decision. She didn't know why her father had come up in her thoughts; he just had, like some kind of vision. With the pressure building around her and feeling like the walls were crumbling, she went back to what she thought was the root of her problems—males abandoning her.

Wanting to look as simple as possible, Luca dressed conservatively in black jeans, a knit sweater, and boots that she'd grabbed from the town's K-mart. Nothing stood out but her beauty.

The crowded visiting room was flooded with a variety of male inmates from H Block and closely watched by a half-dozen strategically positioned correction officers. Luca sat in the middle of it all, in a plastic chair at a small table, her heart beating like a drum.

She set her eyes on the small line of latest inmates coming into the visiting room, single file. She had no idea what her father looked like today. She had only seen a few pictures of him taken over twenty years ago. Would he look the same? Would he recognize her? She fidgeted with her hands as she looked at the six inmates escorted by a solitary guard. One by one, each inmate located his waiting family or friend.

Luca took a deep breath. There was one man left, the last on line. He stood looking around in his khaki prison uniform and work shoes. He was tall with a distinctive look for his imposing physical stature. He looked fit and monastic with his broad mustache and lantern jaw. Luca automatically knew he was her father.

The guard pointed her way, and he nodded.

Luca could see him straining his eyes. She sat upright. She didn't smile or frown. She was utterly uneasy.

Her father slowly came her way.

Luca took a deep breath once again. He had aged well, and he was still a very handsome man, just the way her mother had described him. His dark skin and hazel eyes stood out like snow in the summer. Luca couldn't take her eyes off him.

He came to her table looking surprised. "Luca?"

Luca didn't answer him. She felt herself getting choked up. Should she rise up and greet him with a hug and kiss?

Looking at him, she couldn't control her tears any longer. They trickled down her face like a river. There sat two people with the same DNA but complete strangers to each other.

Her father sat opposite of her, staring in wonder. "I thought I would never see you," he said. "This is really a surprise."

"I don't know what I should call you," Luca replied.

"You can call me whatever you want." He smiled. "You're very beautiful."

She smiled. "Thank you."

It was hard to break the ice between them. Her father was trying. Over twenty years had gone by, and he was rotting away for life in prison for murder. He had no family or friends visiting him.

Travis Roy was a hardcore man trying to now live a peaceful life in one of the roughest prison in the States. His eyes showed a life of trouble, from drug addiction to violence in the streets. But the minute he set them on his daughter, they looked apologetic and loving.

"So what brings you to finally come see me?"

Luca took another deep breath; it felt like she was gasping for air. She locked eyes with him. "I just wanted to see you."

"I'm glad you did. So how you been?"

"I've been okay," she lied.

"You look good, really good . . . a chip off the old block," he joked.

Luca didn't laugh. Nervousness still swallowed her up like darkness in a black hole. She wanted the awkward moment to pass, but it felt like it was going to take some time. "Mama talks about you sometimes," she said.

Travis smiled. "It's been a long time. How is she?"

"She's doing better."

"I'm glad she finally got it right. She deserves better. She deserves happiness. Tell her I said hello."

"I will."

"Any boyfriends, grandkids?"

"No boyfriends, no grandkids."

"You must have the boys going crazy. I always dreamed you would come out so beautiful, and I was right."

Luca vaguely smiled at his remark. There was a moment of silence between them. Both of them were trying to find the right things to say to each other.

"I know your grandmother talks about me," Travis said, smiling, knowing the old woman probably didn't have any good things to say about him.

"She does."

"Well, everything she says about me, it can be crazy, but that was a different life for me."

"I don't judge," Luca said absentmindedly.

"That's good."

Travis gazed at Luca warmly and smiled. "I still can't believe you're actually here. This is the best day of my life, Luca. I'm so glad you came."

"Daddy, why did you leave me?" Luca shot out unexpectedly. She looked like she was about to burst into tears. "Did you not want me?"

"Luca, I never meant to leave you. I'm truly sorry. If I could turn back the hands of time, I would do it different. I allowed my temper to get the best of me. I'm sure your mother told you that I killed a man. That one action stole you away from me for a very long time. I think about you every day . . . what you would look like, how grown up you must've become, what you are doing with your life. And I didn't intentionally leave you. I'm just doing hard time, Luca . . . very hard time. The one thing we can never get back is time. Cherish it, Luca, cherish it and do something with it. Don't waste it like me."

"It hasn't been easy for me out there, you know, with you in here and Mama running the streets."

"I know, baby, and I'm so sorry. But look at you now, you've grown so strong and beautiful. I know you became the better person in the family. Are you in school? Do you have a degree? Are you working?"

Luca didn't want to tell him the truth. She had recently gotten her GED after dropping out of high school like him. She was in the streets and committing worse crimes than her parents could ever imagine. Maybe it was in her genes.

"I'm just surviving, taking things one day at a time."

"Surviving?" Travis repeated, disappointment in his voice. "You shouldn't be surviving, Luca. I know you're better than that."

"How you know what I am?" Luca spat. "You was never around."

Travis lowered his head.

Luca glared at him. "I'm not mad at you. I'm not anymore. There were just times in my life when I felt so alone and needed you around. Why did you have to get sent here? How come I was the one that had to grow up the way I did?"

Travis reached across the table and took her hand into his. "I know I fucked up, Luca. But allow me to be in your life now. You can come visit me whenever, and write me, and I'll write back."

Luca averted her attention away from him, thinking about the troubles in her life. Was it a family curse passed down to her? Why did God bestow such nightmarish shit on her since the day she was born? Many times she felt her life was hell on earth, but she got through the hard times.

"It's easier to make life harder, harder to make life easier," Travis said.

Her father looked like he had all the advice in the world, but none he ever used for himself over twenty years ago.

"Do you forgive me, Luca?"

She connected with his eyes. "I said I'm not mad at you anymore."

"I didn't say if you was mad at me. I asked, do you forgive me? A man named Paul Boese once said, 'Forgiveness does not change the past, but it does enlarge the future.' And you can have a bright future, Luca. But don't become eaten up inside by rage and not forgiving. Don't do it for me, but do it for yourself."

Luca brooded for a moment, looking at him. "I forgive you. I do. I've learned to live without you for a long time."

"Do you want to continue living without me in your life?" he asked, looking apprehensive about her answer. "I want to continue this, Luca. I have nobody else in here. I'm alone."

She wanted to scream out, "You brought this on yourself," but she knew she was only a stone's throw away from following in his footsteps. The life she was living— the murders she ordered, the people she had killed herself, the lives she had destroyed, the people she had poisoned, and the chaos that ensued because of her—how could she judge her father for one mistake when she was making tons of them herself?

"You're not alone, Travis. I'll come back to visit you. I promise."

Her father smiled so broadly, you would think he was being released the following day.

They continued talking, trying to vibe and really get to know each other. He told her stories about his past, but Luca didn't share any of her ill lifestyle with him. She made up lies and veered so far from the truth, she was a different and better person by the end of her story.

Most important, they were bonding. He made her laugh, and he made her think. Travis's intelligence showed, and Luca showed off hers as well. They both were voracious readers.

At the end of their hour visit, Luca felt renewed. Her father wasn't a bad person. Like her, he'd made some poor choices in his life. Talking to him helped her open up to a few things about herself.

"Visit's over," the stocky white guard announced to them sternly.

Neither one of them looked like they wanted to get up and leave.

Travis gazed at his daughter lovingly. He slightly sighed and stood up, stretching across the table. Luca stood up too, and she hugged her father good-bye. Being wrapped in his powerful arms felt good. She had been yearning for her daddy's protection since she was a little girl.

The emotions started to pour in like a flash flood when they began to separate. She watched him walk back to the entrance he'd come out of. He steadily looked back her way and smiled. His look toward her seemed so secure and positive. He got into line with several other inmates and was guided back into maximum security.

Once he was out of sight, Luca's heart dropped. "Daddy!" she cried out, swamped with emotion.

Chapter 7

Phaedra Royce, you made bail," the woman guard shouted out from the other side of the jail bars.

Phaedra, clad in an orange jumpsuit, jumped off the hard prison bench and walked toward the voice of the prison guard. *How did I make bail?*, she said to herself. She couldn't wait to get out of jail, having spent a long, drawn-out two weeks on Rikers Island on a gun charge, along with a few other charges. The judge set her bail at $50,000. She was surprised that the judge actually set a bail for her, with the numerous priors she had.

She followed the hefty female guard from her confined cell, remaining stoic about being released. It wasn't anything she wasn't used to. Rikers Island had been her temporary home on numerous occasions, but she was fortunate that jail never became her permanent home. But with these pending gun charges, her future was starting to look very bleak.

Immediately she started going through the process of being released from Rikers Island. She had no idea who'd footed her $50,000 bail, but she was grateful. Her own money was low because of countless expenses she had picked up living her high-end lifestyle. She didn't want to spend a minute more than she had to in the place considered the biggest prison in the world.

During her last stint on the island she had spent twenty-three hours a day in her cell, in a place they called the "bing" where inmates ended up after making more trouble at the prison. The only time she came out of her cell was for a four-minute shower and for recreation. Phaedra was a hardcore troublemaker during the time she had spent in jail. She cut bitches in the face with razors, fought bitches, and argued with the guards.

Like the streets, prison was never safe. Everywhere there was always a threat. But Phaedra was a banger and a die-hard survivor. She knew that sooner or later she was going to have to do some time for the gun charges. The chances of her beating the charges were thin. It was going to take a good lawyer and prayer for her to come out of this on top. They had her dead to rights.

Phaedra knew she was going down. Two detectives were willing to testify against her. As she was being processed out, she thought about Luca. How could she be so stupid to go after Luca in public? Did she want to get caught? Or did she want to be stopped? She felt like kicking herself. Her mind was spinning.

She had the twisted thought that maybe it was Luca bailing her out so she could track her down and murder her, creating payback in the worst way. The male guard handed Phaedra her personal items, eyeing her up and down. He smiled.

She didn't smile back. With her personal items in hand and back in civilian clothing, she turned around to exit the jail.

The male guard said, "You'll be back. This ain't anything but a revolving door for you." He chuckled.

Phaedra scowled. She wanted nothing more but to spin around and punch him in his face, break his nose maybe. She remembered him from her last stay, and it was obvious that he remembered her. He worked in the female unit and had a reputation for fucking up the young female inmates. She was surprised they hadn't fired him yet.

She kept her cool and walked the opposite way. She had her freedom again, however temporary. There was still a trial or a plea bargain, depending on the prosecutor's call.

Phaedra stepped out of Rikers Island with the sun shining brightly down on her. It was a chilly day, but bearable. She zipped up her coat and looked around. The bus waiting to take her across the bridge was idling and quickly filling up with people ready to leave. She got on board and sat in the back. A minute later, the doors closed, and the bus drove off. She breathed a little easier, but still felt tension at the pit of her stomach.

As they crossed the bridge, she peered out the window, and a smile appeared on her face. There was Meeka standing with the bondsman in the parking lot.

Phaedra hurried off the bus and gave Meeka a prolonged hug.

"Thanks," she said to her friend.

"How you holdin' up?"

"I'm better now."

The bondsman explained the conditions of her bond. He was a six-foot tall, bearded, heavyset white boy who looked like he had been in his profession for years.

Phaedra listened to him talk, but she was ready to go on her way. The conditions of her bond were to appear at all times until full and final disposition of the case, obey all further orders of the bail authority, refrain from criminal activity etc, etc, etc. She had heard it all before. She was hungry and tired and needed someplace comfortable to chill and think.

Phaedra climbed into the passenger seat of Meeka's silver Camry. She wanted to get as far away from the jail as possible. She needed a shower and a gun. Knowing it would be stupid to carry a gun again when she had a pending court case for a gun charge, in her mind, it was better to be judged by twelve than carried by six. And Luca was enemy number one in her book.

As Meeka drove, she glanced at her friend and asked, "What happened?"

"It's a crazy story."

"I got time. Talk to me."

"Have you seen Luca around lately?"

"I called her a few times, but she don't pick up. Something's wrong?"

Phaedra didn't want to tell Meeka, but she needed someone to talk to. Meeka had been out doing her own thing, grinding in the streets, making her own connects and trying to still get money from a crumbling empire. She was smart enough to see the bottom coming up on them, and since Little Bit's and Kool-aid's murders, she went low key. Luca had taught her a lot about finances and investments, and Meeka was trying to play the game smart and do it the right way.

Meeka got on the Grand Central Parkway headed toward the Brooklyn-Queens Expressway doing seventy miles per hour, erratically switching lanes.

Phaedra lit a cigarette and smoked. She gazed out the window and thought about so many things.

Meeka wanted to know what happened with her and Luca.

Phaedra blew out smoke and quickly said, "I fucked up."

"How?"

"I tried to kill her."

Meeka swerved a bit on the highway when she heard it. She shot a look of awe at Phaedra. "You tried to do what?"

"You been out of the loop for a minute, Meeka."

"That's because I'm out here grinding, making money the way Luca taught us how. And you tried to kill her?" Meeka barked. "What the fuck is wrong wit' you, Phaedra?"

"There's nothin' wrong wit' me. You don't know the whole fuckin' story."

"What is the story?"

Phaedra went on to tell Meeka the whole story, from her strong crush on Clyde to Luca coming to the lounge and intervening in her love affair. She went on to say how Luca was changing, becoming a different person.

Phaedra spoke about how Clyde and Luca hooked up and became a couple, and how she was extremely jealous of them. But she also admitted that she once had an obsessive crush on Luca, and still somewhat did. When Luca and Clyde had started fucking, she hated to be around them.

The story continued with Kool-aid being murdered, her emotions on that, and how she ran to Clyde for comfort and support. She had ended up back at his place, and they fucked.

"What is wrong wit' you, Phaedra? Are you dumb or just crazy?"

"Me? You think I'm completely wrong?"

"You all the way fuckin' wrong, Phaedra. First, you is a foul bitch for not only fuckin' Clyde but trying to murder the woman who treated us like family and took us out of the ghetto to prosperity."

"Without us, she wouldn't have any of this shit."

"And without her, we wouldn't either."

Meeka continued to speed toward Brooklyn with a sudden distaste for Phaedra. "You need to make it right," she said.

"Why?"

"Because you need to, that's why."

"I don't need to do shit but stay black and die."

Meeka looked irritated by her response.

Phaedra shouted, "You choosing sides. You going against me, Meeka? That's how it is?"

"You fucked up!"

"I was the one that brought you in," Phaedra shouted, her eyes brimming with anger, "so without me, you wouldn't even fuckin' exist. I fuckin' made you, bitch!"

"You on a sinking fuckin' ship, Phaedra. Realize that. Luca is smart . . . extremely smart. I ain't ever met anyone brilliant like her before. You go against her, who do you think is gonna come out on top? We street thugs, always been and always will, but her, she on a different level. I know I ain't tryin' to reach that high, not even come close. I'm somebody, but I'll never be a genius like her. Understand that, Phaedra. You think I wanna bite the hand that fuckin' feeds me? You crazy, bitch."

Phaedra realized she didn't have anyone in her corner. She was truly alone. If Kool-aid was alive, she knew he would have been on her side. But the girls she'd brought into the business were scared of Luca when she felt they should be afraid of her.

"I never thought you would turn against me," Phaedra said with disdain in her tone. "You can't trust anyone."

"Obviously, you can't," Meeka shot back with a fierce attitude, turning Phaedra's own words against her.

They continued to quarrel in the car.

Meeka made it into Brooklyn and hurried to drop Phaedra off. It was to the point where both girls felt like tearing into each other.

Phaedra smoked her third Newport and was seething. She felt betrayed by everyone, from Clyde, Luca, and Meeka. She was stressed.

Meeka came to a stop in front of a four-story red-brick building on a quiet block in a desolate area of Brooklyn, Phaedra's hush-hush place until things cooled down. Before exiting the car, Phaedra cautiously looked around, making sure she wasn't walking into a setup.

"You need to chill, Phaedra, and don't do anything stupid."

"Now you tellin' me what to fuckin' do?"

"I'm telling you to stay alive."

"Bitch, who the fuck is you to give me advice?"

Phaedra had nothing else to say to Meeka. She climbed out of the idling Camry and stormed toward the entrance to her building.

Meeka drove away cursing loudly.

Phaedra headed into the lobby thinking that any second a bullet was going to pierce her skull. She couldn't help but be nervous. She rushed inside the elevator, pushed for the fourth floor, and rode it with worry.

The minute she walked into her apartment, she went for her stash of guns and removed a .380 and two .45 ACP. She wasn't about to take any chances. She was ready for war.

Chapter 8

The next two days, Phaedra sat around her house depressed. She steadily looked out the window in paranoia like she was working security. She keenly watched every parked car, and if something didn't look right, she was ready to shoot first, no questions asked. She had a gun always in her hand. No one knew about the apartment, besides Meeka, because she had dropped her off. Phaedra had rented it out under a different name and had never frequented the place until now.

She had it furnished with a flat-screen TV, some love seats, cozy chairs, and some modern amenities. She didn't know where to go from here. Her days were spent watching TV and contemplating her next move. She thought about leaving town for a few days, but New York was the only city she knew. She had no family to go to. Luca, Kool-aid, and her crew were the only family she had and loved. Now everyone was either dead or turning against her.

She had only ten thousand dollars saved and an SUV that had been impounded by the NYPD. Things were crumbling around her. Bad Girl was dead, her friendship with Luca was dead, and her hustling days looked like they were about to be dead too.

The only thing Phaedra could do was rebuild something, maybe find her own connect and run her own crew. She didn't care what Meeka said. In her mind, if it wasn't for her, Luca wouldn't be where she was today. It was she who taught Luca the game and how to shoot a gun. She was the one who'd introduced her to her first-cousin Tiffany, and if it wasn't for Tiffany, Luca wouldn't have had the high-end clientele she had today. Phaedra had also recruited the girls and one of the most feared men in the city, Kool-aid, and solidified their loyalty to the organization.

Phaedra was the one catching the bodies out there, strengthening the Bad Girl name and putting fear in hearts. She and Kool-aid got their hands dirty murdering rivals, witnesses, and anyone who crossed Luca or the organization. Luca gave the order; they executed it without any hesitation. Phaedra was Luca's right-hand bitch and would have died for her.

Yes, Luca was a very intelligent and shrewd woman, but she wasn't like the others. She wasn't a thug or street. Phaedra taught her what she needed to know about heroin, for example. Luca was a fast learner and picked up on how to play the game quickly, but Phaedra did most of the dirty work.

Who would have thought it would come to this? Phaedra asked herself.

She walked to the window once again and gazed out. It was a chilly and cloudy evening. Feeling like a hermit, she sighed deeply.

Phaedra pranced around her apartment making phone calls. She tried to call her cousin Tiffany, but her number had changed. She tried to reach some old friends, but to no avail. Either their number had changed, or they weren't picking up.

"I should have stuck with being a dyke," she said to herself.

Loving pussy had its problems too, but when Phaedra jumped on a nigga's dick and started catching feelings for him, it turned her life upside down. She couldn't understand why. What made Clyde so special? Why did she like him so much? She racked her brain to find the reason why.

Her feelings for Clyde came out of nowhere. One day she walked into the Paradise Lounge, took one look at his handsome features, and became stuck on stupid. She started to change up her whole wardrobe, dressing sexier, looking more like a feminine woman than a masculine dyke, and honestly, she started to love the attention—from men and women. She hated to admit it, but Luca did influence her new look. She idolized her boss and wanted to be like her, wanted to love her too. Since Phaedra laid eyes on Luca, she wanted to fuck her.

There were nights when Phaedra's pussy would get soaking wet thinking about passionate nights with Luca. She hungered to sex her down—eat her pussy out, suck on her nipples, and bump pussies with her. The woman was beautiful, and her body was breathtaking. Men became infatuated over Luca. Phaedra craved that same attention.

Growing up, her life was hard, and it was hell. Her last boyfriend, she loved him deeply. When the streets took his life, Phaedra went into shut-down mode for weeks. But she overcame her grief and dealt with the loss and came back into her own, which never was much. She was plagued with many bad memories, from the violent loss of her boyfriend when she was fifteen years old to being in and out of abusive foster homes from as far back as she could remember.

Phaedra sat by her bedroom window and started to roll up a blunt. She needed to smoke, she needed to escape. She wanted her mind to drift somewhere different. As she placed the blunt between her lips and gazed out the window, she thought about her parents. Never knowing her mother was a disheartening feeling, and her father being killed when she was only two years old only added to her pain.

The first time one of her foster parents tried to sexually abuse her, she was eight years old. The first time she had sex, she was eleven years old. Her mentally disturbed foster brother held her down on the bed and forcefully penetrated her, breaking her virginity and raping her. He was fifteen. From there, it was always some pervert drooling over her developing, young body. All her life, she fought them off. Most battles she won, while there were a few she lost.

Phaedra inhaled and then exhaled loudly. She thought about how her prior boyfriend was gunned down while sitting in a parked car on Fulton Street. Rocky was once the love of her life. In fact, Clyde reminded her of him. He was tall and dark. Rocky was nineteen with a dark goatee like Clyde's and a strong physique like his. She missed him and thought about him all the time. Clyde and Rocky definitely had similar traits. They both didn't take shit from anyone, and they both were leaders.

Phaedra had never told Luca how she truly felt about her. And once Clyde's love had been diverted elsewhere, she felt like she had made the same mistake again.

Thinking about her past, her beef with Luca, her mistakes with Clyde, losing Kool-aid, and Meeka turning against her stirred about some sudden and troubling emotions inside of her.

She continued puffing on the blunt and felt her eyes watering. She was gangsta, no denying that, but at the end of the day, she was still a woman with emotions. She never felt so alone in her entire life. Even growing up in foster care and group homes, she always had somebody or something to turn to, be it a gang, or a boyfriend or girlfriend to comfort her when she was down. Now it seemed like her future was a dead end. She was trying so hard not to let it be.

Fearing Luca may have put a contract on her life, she felt she had to make the first move. She had to lay low for a moment and come up with a plan. Meeka saying that Luca was smart and brilliant was true, but Phaedra had been surviving on her own since she was a little girl. Luca wasn't built like her. Luca didn't come up like her. The bitch was a soft, naïve girl who grew up in the ghetto, but she wasn't ghetto. She ran more than she fought.

As Phaedra was finishing off her blunt, trying to come up with a solution to her twisted life, her cell phone rang. She stared at it suspiciously, not knowing the number calling her. She answered the call warily, holding her breath, thinking it was Luca or someone from the organization. Not too many people had her cell phone number.

"Who the fuck is this?" she answered.

"Phaedra, don't hang up. It's me, Clyde."

Hearing his voice, her breath felt short, and she became apprehensive. Why was he calling her? Shocked, she remained quiet.

"Phaedra, are you still there?"

"I'm here," she replied with terseness.

"I want to see you."

"See me? Why?"

"It's important."

It was a surprise to her, his asking her to come see him. At first, she thought Luca had gotten Clyde to set her up to be murdered. She didn't trust him or the situation. It seemed too weird. Clyde loved Luca. Why did he want her to come see him? It bothered Phaedra greatly.

"What about Luca?" she asked.

"She's no longer a factor in my life. I got rid of her."

"Rid of her?" she asked, confused. "You killed her?"

"No, I dumped her."

"Why?" Now it definitely didn't make sense to Phaedra. *What the fuck is going on?* she screamed inside of her head.

"I can't stop thinking about you, Phaedra. That night we made love, it was the best feeling I ever had. I was lying to myself when I got with Luca. The minute I saw you walking into my place, I was attracted to you, but I thought the man you was with, I assumed the two of y'all were together. I didn't want to interfere. So I focused my attention on Luca. She's a beautiful woman, but she's not for me."

Phaedra heard him talking, but it was still difficult to believe him. It could be a setup. She was going through an array of emotions. She felt so vulnerable at the moment, she didn't know if she was walking into a trap. Clyde could be lying through his teeth. He and Luca both were brilliant and manipulative people. They didn't get to the top by being stupid. They knew how to use people—how to make them believe in them and trust them.

Her heart was willing to take the chance. She was in love with Clyde. When he woke up from his brief coma and called out Luca's name, it crushed her. She thought she would never see or speak to him again.

"I tried calling your phone for days, but I kept getting the voice mail. What happened to you? Where have you been?" he asked.

Either he didn't know, or he was pretending not to know that she had made an attempt on Luca's life and was on Rikers Island with a gun charge lingering over her head.

Did Luca tell him? If not, then why not? So many questions ran through Phaedra's head. "I've been busy," she lied.

"We need to talk in person."

Phaedra was willing to have a talk with him, but it was risky. Her heart ached to see him, but was she putting her life on the line? Was it all fabricated to create her demise?

"I'll come see you."

"That's good, Phaedra. Thank you."

She wasn't going alone. She planned on taking along a friend with her, just in case things weren't what they appeared to be.

***

Phaedra got out of the gypsy cab dressed like an African goddess, wearing a cinnamon-colored skirt that hung low on her hips and a V-neck T-shirt that fit close enough to show off all her assets but wasn't at all vulgar. Covering her shapely body was a chic coat to shield her from the winter cold.

She strutted into the hospital concealing the .45 ACP in her purse. It was fully loaded and already cocked back. Every step she took to Clyde's room was a cautious one. She was very observant, watching everything and everyone, and tremendously nervous. There could be killers waiting around the corner to strike at any time.

However, her biggest threat was catching another gun charge. If she got knocked again and caught a second gun charge, there wasn't going to be any bail this time. It was straight to jail for a minimum of two to five years.

But she couldn't stay away from Clyde. There was something strong about him that made her take the risk. She felt he was the love of her life. She hoped he wasn't lying and was genuine with his feelings.

Phaedra stepped off the elevator and made her way toward his room. The floor was busy with staff and patients. Everything seemed normal. No one paid her any attention.

She walked into Clyde's room. He was awake; sitting up and watching TV. He looked much better. When he saw her standing in the doorway looking hesitant, a smile appeared on his face, and he invited her inside.

"I'm here."

"I'm glad you made it." Clyde couldn't take his eyes off her.

She looked around the room, and it seemed empty.

"She's not here, and I'm not trying to set you up."

"How do I know that?"

"Because she threatened my life too."

She locked eyes with him. He seemed sincere, but no one could ever tell. "What did you say to her?"

"What needed to be said."

"And why now?"

"Because Luca and I may be cut from the same cloth, but I know honestly, she will never be there for me the way I'm going to need her. She's running an empire, I'm a paraplegic now. This is my second time shot multiple times and lying in the hospital. I survived it then, and I'm going to survive it now."

Phaedra stepped closer to him, her eyes lingering on his condition. It saddened her too. He couldn't walk, but he seemed strong. She pulled the chair beside his bed and took a seat in it. "What do you want from me?" she asked him.

"I want to love you. I need you, Phaedra. I need you badly." His eyes softened, and his voice carried great weight. "I know I can't do this without you."

Phaedra took his hand into hers and sighed. She couldn't refuse him. She couldn't turn away from him. If it was a lie, then it would be the best lie ever told, and she would be the biggest fool for falling victim to it. But his eyes spoke some truth, and his tone sounded needy, or so she wanted to believe.

She looked at him. "What do you need me to do?"

Phaedra, who had once lost trust in men, fell deeply in love with him, thinking he chose her over Luca out of pure love. Had she listened with her head and not her heart, she would have heard exactly what he said: He chose her because he *needed* her, not because he loved her. Phaedra was ready to play wifey and do whatever he needed to get him back to one hundred percent. She was ready to start a new chapter in her life. And hopefully a great one.

Chapter 9

K'wan crossed the Tri-Boro Bridge that led into 125th Street in Harlem, on his way to meet with the infamous World. Dwayne, very happy to be home, was riding shotgun. K'wan's reunion with his little brother was a merry one. He thought he would never see him again.

K'wan hugged him briefly. "That snitch, Roscoe, he's fuckin' expired."

Dwayne smiled. "I knew you would take care of it fo' me, big bro."

"You know I would."

Dwayne sat smugly in the car, feeling untouchable by his brother's side. K'wan always came through for him, no matter what obstacle it was—Batman and Robin, the Dynamic Duo.

The blood of over two dozen bodies was on their hands. The ghetto was calling the brothers the "Teflon thugs," because they seemed to be untouchable to federal and state prosecution. K'wan had been acquitted a half dozen times, and Dwayne managed to beat his most trying indictment yet. He still had a trial looming, but he was confident that the state didn't have any hard evidence against him. Besides, his lawyer was positive they wouldn't go to trial, especially now without any witnesses. With so many loopholes in the justice system, Dwayne had found a shrewd attorney to try and squirm his way toward an acquittal.

K'wan's black-on-black Dodge Charger merged with the heavy traffic on 125th Street. The area was flooded with shoppers, pedestrians, and vehicles.

Dwayne lit a cigarette, his eyes transfixed on a big-booty woman in tight jeans crossing the intersection in front of them. He exhaled the cigarette smoke and said, "Damn, that shit right there is nice, yo. She got a phat ass. I need some of that right now."

"You need to stay focused. Fuck that bitch!" K'wan spat.

"Yeah, fuck that bitch. That's what I'm talkin'bout. She gettin' my dick hard too."

"You a fuckin' trip, nigga."

Dwayne laughed.

They proceeded toward the west side of Harlem, going to the housing projects on Amsterdam Avenue. Their meeting with World was in an hour, but K'wan wanted to get there early and scope out the surroundings to make sure it wasn't a setup. Apart from his brother, everyone was a potential threat.

As K'wan drove, he looked around the area. If it wasn't Brooklyn, he hated it. Stopped at a red light, he hooked his attention on three young goons exiting a clothing store carrying a few shopping bags. They were flashy and covered in bling, looking like drug dealers.

"Fuck these Harlem niggas. They think they run the fuckin' world."

Dwayne didn't comment on K'wan's words. He simply glanced at him.

K'wan continued with, "How well you know this nigga World?"

"I was locked up wit' his boy, Doc. We were tight in Rikers back in the days. He saved my life. I met World twice. He's a serious muthafucka, K'wan."

"What? You think we ain't?"

"I'm sayin', he from Brooklyn, and I heard he's connected wit' some big-time muthafuckas."

Hearing that the man was from Brooklyn caught K'wan off guard. "Brooklyn?" he uttered, bewilderment plastered across his face.

"Yeah, he from the 'Ville. He came into Harlem and took over this bitch. Pushed some big-time drug dealer named Squirrel off his fuckin' throne and got his name ringing out this bitch."

K'wan was listening. It didn't matter where he was from, he still had his doubts. What did a man with that much power want with a local stickup kid?

The brothers made it to the west side and parked across the street from the sprawling housing project on Amsterdam Avenue. The area was busy with residents.

"So, we just gon' sit back and wait?" Dwayne asked.

"Yeah, fo' a minute, just check out the area and see what's good."

Dwayne shrugged.

They both were armed with pistols. Dwayne wasn't in the mood to wait, but K'wan had been a goon for too long for him not to trust his judgment.

K'wan lit a cigarette and looked at everything, from the simplest person crossing the street to watching the car drive by with the heavy bass blaring. He'd done too many stickups to not know what to look out for, especially if he felt a setup was about to happen.

"So this Doc nigga, what he about?" K'wan asked.

"He dead."

K'wan raised his eyebrow. "Why he dead?"

"He got shot down by Squirrel's peoples in the club a few months back."

"And you think gettin' down wit' this nigga is good fo' business wit' us?"

"I'm just sayin' bro, I ain't scared or anything, but this nigga World, I heard stories about him from Doc and a few other muthafuckas that are 'bout that murder game, and to tell you the truth, I rather be on his good side than his bad," Dwayne stated coolly.

K'wan chuckled. "You think he the bogeyman or somethin'?"

"Close to it."

"Fuck that!" K'wan said. "We meet this nigga, I feel him out, and if he flinches wrong in my direction, I'm blasting him."

Dwayne heard his brother talking, but he knew if shit went wrong, it wasn't going to be that easy. But no matter what happened, he still had his brother's back.

The brothers smoked and chilled for a half hour, talking and watching everything around them before K'wan gestured that it was time. They exited the car and walked across the busy avenue, 9 mms tucked snugly in their waistbands. They walked into the towering projects like they owned the place. Knowing they were a long way from Brooklyn, the brothers kept their hands near their weapons—cocked back and safeties already off—in case of trouble.

K'wan moved casually, and Dwayne followed behind him. They walked by residents coming and going, but the cold kept almost everyone indoors. When they walked into the lobby of the building, there was a dice game happening in the corner. Three young men were huddled over a few scattered tens and twenties on the floor, drinking Hennessy, and talking shit to each other.

When K'wan and Dwayne walked in they briefly caught attention, and a few hard looks were exchanged, but nothing serious happened.

K'wan pushed for the elevator and waited. Time was passing by too slow for him. The sooner he met with World and left back for Brooklyn, the better.

Ding. The elevator stopped at the lobby, and the metal doors slid back into the walls.

The brothers stepped into the foul, pissy-smelling box and pushed for the eleventh floor. They ascended in silence, their minds spinning with their own thoughts and worries.

Exiting from the elevator onto the eleventh floor, they heard rap music blaring from an apartment. There was a young mother leaving out her apartment pushing her infant son in a stroller toward the elevator. She gave K'wan and Dwayne a fleeting look as she passed by them.

Dwayne gazed back at her plump booty decorated with tight Juicy sweat pants and smiled.

K'wan nudged Dwayne and barked, "Stay focused, nigga! Fuckin' pussy always got you distracted."

"I've been down fo' a minute. You forgot?"

"It ain't been that fuckin' long. You ain't do no bid."

"Whatever, K'wan."

They stopped at the apartment at the end of the hallway. They were ten minutes early. K'wan knocked and waited. The door to the neighboring apartment opened, and out stepped a goon with a double-pump shotgun and a scowl.

K'wan kept his cool, as did Dwayne.

"Who the fuck is y'all niggas?" the man asked.

"We here to see World," K'wan replied.

"Why World wanna see y'all niggas?"

"Because he asked fo' us. Is that a problem, nigga?" K'wan wanted to make it clear that he wasn't intimidated by the shotgun and definitely not the man.

The man continued scowling. He stepped farther out of the apartment and knocked on the next door with the bottom of his fist while still sizing them up.

"It's Beat Man. Open up," he hollered.

K'wan and Dwayne stood aside and watched. They both wondered what kind of bizarre operation they were walking into.

The second apartment door opened, and a muscular man clad in a wife-beater, red bandanna covering his face, and a pistol tucked into his jeans stood in front of them. He eyed the brothers. "Fuck y'all niggas want wit' World?"

K'wan hissed, "What the fuck is this? Where's fuckin' Waldo?"

The thug glared at the brothers, and K'wan returned the same menacing stare. Muscles and a gun didn't scare him.

Dwayne interrupted the stare-down. "We don't mean any disrespect, but we here 'bout business. Tell ya boss K'wan and Dwayne showed up. Like my brother said, he's expecting us."

The man looked at Dwayne and then got on the horn to inform his boss the hitters from Brooklyn had arrived. When he got the okay, without apology, he stepped to the side and allowed the brothers into the apartment.

The brothers walked into a mini drug factory. Half a million dollars in heroin was being packaged for street distribution by topless woman seated at a table wearing latex gloves, as armed thugs lingered everywhere.

K'wan and Dwayne stood in the center of the room and waited. When one of World's soldiers attempted to pat him down, K'wan immediately lifted his shirt, revealing the gun he had on him, and sternly said, "Nigga, do what you want, but this joint ain't leaving my side."

The soldier looked upset.

K'wan wasn't about to budge. Dwayne followed his brother's lead, arguing to stay strapped too.

When it looked like a confrontation was about to ensue between the soldier and the brothers, a voice boomed out, "Marko, chill out and let them keep their toys. They ain't no threat," and the soldier backed off.

World walked into the room shirtless, his body decorated with menacing-looking tattoos and war scars. He locked eyes with K'wan, and instantly real recognized real.

"I heard some good things 'bout you," World said. "And I know you heard the nightmares about me."

"I heard things, but they don't scare me," K'wan replied in a temperate tone. "But thanks for bailing my little brother out."

"It's the least I could do. Doc used to talk highly of your brother."

"I'm sorry he's gone," Dwayne chimed.

"That's the game, my nigga—shit happens."

"So what's happening here?" K'wan spoke. "We ain't here on a social call to talk about reputations."

World chuckled. "I respect that . . . a man 'bout his business and ain't tryin' to waste time."

World looked at one of his goons. The man nodded and reached into a book bag.

K'wan keenly kept his eyes on him.

The man pulled out a small bundle of money and tossed it at K'wan and Dwayne. K'wan caught it in mid-air.

"That's twenty-five thousand to start," World said.

"Start what?"

"I want you to come work for my organization. I need killers like you on my team. As you can see, I pay my goons really good. I'm a rich fuckin' man, K'wan, and you can be rich too."

"You serious?"

"I don't play games." World gazed at the brothers. He seemed cold as space.

K'wan glanced at Dwayne, who shrugged.

"I know you were once a king in your hood, and someone took that throne away from you. K'wan, we got the same enemy, and that same enemy is my cousin, Luca."

"Bad Girl took over my shit," K'wan said.

"Yeah, I know, and I control Bad Boy."

"You?"

It suddenly hit K'wan. World was also a competitor on the streets. K'wan scowled.

World went on to say, "The enemy of my enemy is my friend, right? Let bygones be bygones, K'wan, and join the family. We could use you and ya brother."

K'wan stood there contemplating the proposition. He was a killer, but he wasn't any fool. He found himself surrounded by killers and in a hard place, deep in foreign territory.

Dwayne stood silently next to his brother. K'wan's choice was also his choice.

K'wan looked at the twenty-five thousand dollars in his hand. It was easy money. His brother was home, and he was being paid to do something he would do for free.

"So, what's ya answer, K'wan? You can leave here a rich man or a poor man."

K'wan was thirsty for power and he saw it in World. "I love money," he told World.

World smiled. "Welcome to the family, my nigga."

Chapter 10

Phaedra walked into the Paradise Lounge in SoHo and looked around. The place was closed until Clyde got back on his feet. He was losing business and needed someone he could trust to run it.

Phaedra told him that she didn't have any experience managing a lounge. Why the fuck did he pick her, when there were other qualified employees ready to take the reins? But Clyde was persistent. He, for some reason, fully trusted her.

She had moved into his well-furnished brownstone to be at his beck and call. After his release from the hospital several weeks after the shooting, he needed twenty-four-hour care.

Phaedra was there to help him every step of the way. She was growing up and felt herself becoming a different woman. The transition was difficult, but she really liked taking care of Clyde and being there for him.

All her life, she had never had a real home, a place to call her own, and someone to truly love her. Staying in

Clyde's lavish brownstone made her feel like a queen—it made her feel useful.

She walked around the lounge and looked around. She took a deep breath and sat by the bar. The lights were on, but no one was around. She was the only one inside. She had her own key to the establishment and had to figure out how to run this place without Clyde being around to help her. He'd told her to give him a call if she had any questions on anything, no matter how big or small the issue.

Phaedra decided the place needed cleaning. She took out the mop and bucket and washed the floors, then wiped down the tables, cleaned the bar, and more. It was a tedious job, but she got it done. She wanted to be a part of it. She wanted a change, to see what life felt like without a gun. She felt good, all while watching her back, thinking Luca was going to strike at any time.

She didn't tell Clyde about the gun charge she had caught. She had an upcoming court date, but her attorney had plans to postpone it as long as possible. The threat of serving jail time lingered in her mind.

Clyde had his secrets too. The doctors had told him it was going to take years of physically therapy for him to get right. He knew he couldn't do it alone, and so he picked Phaedra, knowing she was the more vulnerable one. Luca was his equal, and being a drug queenpin with an attempt on her life, she probably wouldn't be around for the long haul. Nor was he sure that Luca could fully forgive him for sleeping with her best friend, and his indiscretion would always be the elephant in the room. Clyde cared deeply for Phaedra, but he wasn't in love with her. He only wanted her around to help take care of him and help manage his home and his business. He was still in love with Luca.

***

Phaedra stood behind the bar watching the crowd, feeling like a fish out of water. This wasn't her element. From a rough Brooklyn neighborhood to an affluent lounge in SoHo, she felt like she went through a portal and came out a different person. A year ago, she wouldn't have recognized her own self. The transformation was dramatic. She was ready to try anything for love.

With the help of Clyde's employees, within a week she started getting the hang of things, learning the bar, learning how to manage the lounge, and becoming familiar with the regulars who came through to have a few drinks and a wonderful time. She was a fast learner, and actually liked the new life she was living. It wasn't a secret that she and Clyde were a couple, and if the employees at Paradise Lounge resented it, they didn't show it.

Every night, while on her way home to her new man via cab, Phaedra moved cautiously from point A to point B. Luca was out there, lurking somewhere, so she didn't feel safe. She carried her pistol everywhere with the mentality that it was either Luca or her.

At the brownstone, she cooked, cleaned, and encouraged Clyde to keep his spirits up. She was home when the physical therapist came to work with him on his rehabilitation, and at nights she was running Paradise. After two weeks the place was starting to see a profit again.

"You are a good woman, Phaedra," Clyde said.

She smiled. "Thank you. I'm here for you, and I will always be here for you."

Clyde yearned for Luca night and day as he strived for recovery. But he'd made a choice, one he felt would benefit him most. Luca was his love, but Phaedra was a business decision; one he hoped he wouldn't regret.

Chapter 11

Luca's trip upstate to see her father was an emotional one. She stayed one week and went to see him a second time. The second visit was a better visit. Father and daughter tried to get more in tune with each other, talking and laughing. Travis didn't appear to be the monster her grandmother portrayed him to be. His eyes were kind and caring. He'd made a mistake a long time ago and was paying heavily for it. He regretted the thirty seconds that changed his life forever. He expressed himself deeply, steadily apologizing to the one girl who truly mattered.

Luca made it back to Brooklyn late in the night. She had left all her tears in upstate New York and was determined not to fall apart. Now was the time to rebuild. What didn't kill her would only make her stronger, and she yearned to become stronger. She needed to put together a new team, to exact the revenge she was yearning for. The Kabakoff brothers had violated her in the worst way by burning down her house with her money and drugs inside. The only one she could now trust to put them in their graves and make shit happen was Meeka.

She parked, removed the pistol from her handbag, and climbed out the car. She kept her pistol close as she walked toward her grandmother's building with extreme caution, knowing nowhere was ever safe. The ghetto was quiet tonight. The hustlers were out partying, splurging their drug money, and the fiends had faded from the area, like yesterday. The residents were cooped up in their apartments, trying to stay warm on a chilly night.

Luca didn't plan to stay in Brownsville long. She was ready to be in and out like a minute-man in the bedroom. Quickly, she went into the building and took the stairs to her floor. She hurried into the apartment, checked in on her grandmother, and went into her bedroom. Luca sat at the foot of her bed weighing her options. She had already spoken to Meeka about the business she needed her to tend to, and Meeka promised she would get it done.

Now it was about money. She was ready to sell the Audi, her jewelry, and anything valuable. With all her drug money and product burned down to the ground, now was the time to get in contact with her attorney. Dominic was her only hope. She had called and left a zillion messages, but when he didn't answer or return her calls, worry started to set in.

After the umpteenth phone call went unanswered, she screamed into the phone, cursing him out and calling him every bad name in the book. The last message she left him was, "Nigga, you better have my fuckin' money right, because I'll be at your office first thing tomorrow morning."

It was first on Luca's agenda. Monday morning she was packing her pistol and going to see Dominic unannounced. If he fucked her over, she had nothing to lose, and she wasn't going down without a fight.

But tonight she needed to rest. It had been a long and lonely drive back from upstate New York. Luca undressed, stripping down to her panties and bra, and slid herself underneath the covers to a warm bed. Closing her eyes, she thought about her father. The last thing she wanted was to end up like him, doing hard time in prison, or end up dead like Naomi. She had to be methodical with every step, like moving through a large field with landmines buried everywhere. One step—*Boom!*—and pieces of her would be everywhere.

***

Luca strutted into the towering downtown skyscraper like a bitch ready for war. She wore a business suit to handle her business. Luca stormed through the lobby and went straight to the elevator. She had a strong feeling that Dominic was ignoring her calls. She hurried off the elevator and toward his office.

The minute she walked through the doors, his receptionist immediately announced from behind her desk, "Luca, he isn't in today."

"Fuck that! I need to see him." She hurried past the receptionist's desk and charged into his office only to find that his receptionist was right. It looked like he hadn't been inside his office for a while.

The receptionist came behind Luca. "I said he isn't in today."

Luca spun around and glared at the bimbo-looking blonde-haired woman. "So where the fuck is he?"

"He's out of town."

"To where, and for how fuckin' long?"

"I can't divulge that information, ma'am."

"Bitch, you know my name, and I need to know where my fuckin' attorney is. This is really fuckin' important."

"I'll try and get word to him that you came by."

"Fuck that shit!" Luca spat. "I need to get word to him now, and I'm not going any fuckin' where until you get his ass on the fuckin' phone."

The leggy receptionist didn't want any trouble from Luca. She was aware of her violent and dangerous reputation. It clearly frightened her that Luca was in the office ranting and carrying on. Luca wasn't the only client upset with Dominic's latest business practices. The receptionist had been receiving phone calls all day from dissatisfied clients eagerly asking to see him.

"I would like to help, but my hands are tied, Luca. Mr. Sirocco didn't leave me a forwarding number to reach him, and I truly have no idea about his whereabouts," she explained. "And I'm afraid if you don't leave here now, I'm going to have to call security to remove you."

Luca shifted her weight to one side, her hands on her hip, staring at the bitch fiercely. She smirked. "Look who grew some fuckin' balls. Bitch, you threatening me?"

"I just don't want any trouble."

"There won't be any trouble if I speak to Dominic."

"Look, the best I could do for you is—"

"No, the best you can do for me is take down my personal number, and the minute he comes through that door, you fuckin' call me."

The receptionist nodded. She took down Luca's number and placed it on her desk.

"And if I hear he's back in town and I don't receive a fuckin' phone call from you soon then, bitch, it won't be pretty for you. And, yes, that is a fuckin' threat—Fuck with me, bitch!"

Luca pushed past her and stormed out of the office, the frustration of being played and lied to manifested on her face. She hurried out the building and walked to her car.

She climbed into her car and lingered for a moment. She picked up her cell phone, scrolled down her call list, and dialed Meeka's number. She was handing out threats, but she needed to back them up too. She couldn't look weak, even though the hand she held at the card table was weak and she couldn't bluff for too long.

Luca needed a strong team of killers. Meeka had the task Phaedra once had of recruiting people to work for her. The only solid thing Luca still had going for her was the blackmailing and extortion of judges, police officers, lawyers, and politicians. She had all of their transgressions locked away in a safety deposit box in the city. If push came to shove, she had that card in her back pocket.

The phone rang several times before Meeka finally answered.

"What's the verdict?" Luca asked, not beating around the bush.

"In Brooklyn now, and I'm about to talk to someone at the moment, Luca," Meeka said.

"I'm depending on this, Meeka. Make it happen."

"I will, Luca."

Luca ended the call.

Meeka was the only one she could depend on right now. With her team fading, it felt like the well was finally running dry.

Luca locked eyes with herself in the rearview mirror and sighed intensely. She lit a cigarette. She remembered a time when she was no one, a bitch without a future, and it felt like the world was constantly taking a shit on her. She was the people's toilet. With her fierce attitude now, it was hard to ever think she was meek, scared of her own shadow. The difference now was that she'd had a taste of power and wealth, and she wanted more. She would die before she ever went back to being that scared, naïve, stupid bitch again.

She finished her cigarette and flicked it out the window. Getting a fierce crew was relevant to rebuilding her empire. Her ship wasn't sinking yet.

***

Meeka climbed out of her silver Camry parked on Myrtle Avenue and gazed at the Marcy Houses in Brooklyn. The notorious housing project, once home to Jay-Z and Memphis Bleek, was teeming with residents enjoying the rare winter day of warm sunshine and fifty-five-degree weather after freezing rain and bitter cold. Meeka hit the pavement in her black and white Nikes, dark jeans, and pullover hoodie covering her long cornrows, looking more like a female roughneck than a young lady. She carried a loaded 9 mm on her person with the safety off, ready for anyone and anything.

She briskly walked toward the six-story brick building. Passing a few thugs and hustlers, she moved with purpose as she entered the lobby. She was going to visit a friend she thought would benefit the organization. They needed hardcore people who didn't give a fuck and would strike fear on the streets. Her friend was Brooklyn, a nineteen-year-old perpetual troublemaker recently released from prison for aggravated assault and battery, drug possession, and resisting arrest. Since she was fifteen years old when she had incurred the felony charges, she was tried as a minor and did three and a half years.

Meeka took the elevator to the sixth floor, stepped off, and walked toward the apartment, hoping her friend was home. She knocked on the door of the apartment with the rap music blaring and the strong smell of weed coming from behind the door. She knocked harder and waited.

After a minute of waiting, she heard someone answering the door. When it opened, a bald man in a soiled wife-beater appeared in front of her, his belly protruding and tattoos showing. He had no-good written all over him.

"What the fuck you want?" he asked.

"Brooklyn. Is she here?" Meeka asked, scowling him.

"What the fuck you want wit' my daughter?"

"Just to talk."

He looked Meeka up and down, sizing her up, looking like a slob and a pervert. He reeked of nastiness and disgust. He purposely blocked Meeka's entrance into the apartment. "Brooklyn ain't here," he said.

"Look, you stupid muthafucka, I ain't here to play fuckin' games. I know Brooklyn just came home, and I need to see her."

He shot back, "You threatening me at my crib? Yeah, I remember you. You were a little ho back in the days, weren't you? You still that ho? Yeah, I bet you still are." He chuckled.

Meeka frowned.

"My daughter—"

"Step-daughter," she corrected him, knowing he didn't care for Brooklyn at all. He was a lowlife and a bum who'd shacked up with Brooklyn's mother years ago, leeching off her benefits and food stamps. He'd never had a job and didn't have any ambition at all, except for trying to get into young girls' panties.

"You need to stay away," he warned.

"Or what?"

"You think 'cuz you older now that you big and bad, bitch? I'll still snatch you into this crib, bend you over my knee, pull ya panties down, and smack that ass."

Meeka glared at him, smirked, quickly pulled out the 9 mm, and pointed it at him.

He jumped back. "Oh, so it's like that now?"

"You a stupid muthafucka that gotta make shit difficult. I just came by lookin' for Brooklyn, and now you 'bout to have me catch a fuckin' murder charge. Where is she?"

"Brooklyn ain't here," he said submissively.

That made Meeka angrier. "I should shoot ya fuckin' dumb ass."

He cringed, staring down the barrel of the gun. "Ain't no disrespect."

"Yeah, you ain't talkin' that shit now. Where is she?" Meeka asked through clenched teeth.

"She left an hour ago."

Meeka felt like shooting him just for being an asshole, but he wasn't worth her time. Seeing the nigga cower like a bitch was thrilling enough.

"Next time I waste my time wit' you, the last thing you gonna hear is that fuckin' pop. Don't fuck wit' me, nigga!"

Meeka hurried back to her car. She wasn't about to give up on finding Brooklyn. Knowing her friend, she was trying to find weed and then some dick. Three and a half years was a long time to go without either.

She climbed into her Camry. She knew all the weed spots in Bed-Stuy and Brownsville. She observed Brooklyn exiting the two-story corner brownstone on Lewis Avenue. Traffic at the brownstone was continuous, in and out with various people; making it known something illegal was happening. Meeka smiled seeing her homegirl again.

Brooklyn still looked the same after three years being incarcerated. She was five five, black like tar, her raven-black hair styled into two long pigtails, eyes black as ink, and plump in the back. She got the name Brooklyn because her mother gave birth to her in the backseat of a car on a Brooklyn block during a snowstorm, right after turning a trick. Her mother felt if the Brooklyn streets couldn't kill her daughter during birth, then she was born to run the rough and tough borough someday.

Meeka drove toward Brooklyn as she walked with a cigar nestled behind her ear and smoking a cigarette. Brooklyn walked like she had somewhere urgent to go, moving fast, puffing on her cancer stick. She didn't notice the Camry approaching her until it was riding parallel to her as she walked.

"Yo, shorty, what's good? Let me get that number," Meeka joked, trying to sound like a thirsty male hollering at her from the car.

Brooklyn gave her the middle finger. "Fuck off!"

"Oh, so it's like that, Brooklyn? That's how you treat an old friend?" Meeka said, no longer trying to disguise her voice.

Brooklyn stopped walking and shot a look at the car. Realizing who was behind the wheel, her frown turned into a smile.

"Oh shit! Is that my muthafuckin' bitch, Meeka?"

"You know it, bitch."

Brooklyn was impressed by the Camry. The paint job and rims stood out like an all-star on Rucker's court.

Meeka put the vehicle in park and jumped out. She immediately hugged her friend.

"I heard you was doin' it big out here, Meeka. Shit! Bitches weren't lying." Brooklyn continued to admire the Camry, looking inside, touching the interior. "How can I get one of these?"

"Fuck wit' me, easily."

"Hey, I need to make some ends, fo' real."

The girls gazed at each other cheerfully, ready to catch up on long-lost time between them.

"It's good to see you home."

"I'm glad to be finally home. Bitch feel free as a fuckin' bird now."

"I went by ya crib, almost shot ya fuckin' stepfather," Meeka said.

"That clown-ass nigga. I wish you did. I ain't been home a week yet, and he already startin' wit' his shit."

"Give the word, and I can make it happen."

"Damn! You got cold like that?"

"You don't even know the half of it."

Brooklyn nodded her head in approval. In her eyes, Meeka was always hard core, a street brawler, a fighter down for whatever, but she had not yet transformed into a killer. Brooklyn didn't know Meeka had graduated to a murderous enforcer when she got down with Luca.

Rumors of Brooklyn catching two bodies before her three and a half-year incarceration had circulated throughout the hood. They said she had bodied two niggas for her man when he caught a corner beef with some rivals over some cash and a few vials. Detectives came at her intensely, but she didn't crack, sticking to her story. Due to insufficient evidence and lack of witnesses, the murder case against her became a cold case file.

"Where you goin'?" Meeka asked.

"Yo, check this, I been home less than a week, and already I got bitches talkin' shit 'bout me. I know where this bitch rest at, so I'm gonna stop by and just have a talk wit' her. You know, let a bitch know I'm home and warn her to keep my name out her fuckin' mouth."

"You need a ride?"

"Bitch, you read my fuckin' mind."

The two ladies climbed into the car, and Meeka headed to where Brooklyn wanted to go.

"So who you down wit', Meeka?"

"I roll wit' a tight crew, and it's run by a bitch."

"Oh, word?"

"She's smart and vicious, and she took over the hood wit' some quality dope. It pays to be on her team, Brooklyn. I'm out here grindin' and getting' my paper up." Meeka reached into her pocket and pulled out a wad of hundreds.

Brooklyn's eyes lit up. "Damn, bitch! What? You the Rockefeller of the hood?"

"Tryin' to be."

Stopped at a red light, Meeka peeled a few hundred-dollar bills from her wad and handed them to Brooklyn. "Consider it a welcome-home gift."

Brooklyn took the $400. "Shit, bitch! I knew there was a reason we always got along."

Meeka laughed. She didn't need to persuade hard. The light changed to green, and Meeka drove off with a grin, knowing the recruitment was going well.

Three blocks later, Brooklyn fixed her stare out the window and shouted, "There go that fuckin' bitch right there."

Meeka sped toward the curb, and before her car could come to a complete stop, Brooklyn leaped out and quickly lunged for the brown-skinned girl clad in gang attire and a red bandanna.

"You talkin' shit, bitch!" Brooklyn screamed out, striking first, punching her rival in the face over and over.

Meeka hopped out her car and helped her friend beat the girl down. Brooklyn had the girl's long hair entangled around her fist and tore into her face savagely with blow after blow, causing the girl to stumble and cry out. Meeka got her hits off too. When the girl dropped to the pavement in a fetal position, they kicked and stomped her repeatedly.

"I'm home now, bitch! Keep talkin'! Keep fuckin' talkin'!" Brooklyn shouted heatedly. "I told you keep my fuckin' name out ya fuckin' mouth."

The girl's blood spewed onto the concrete, her teeth kicked in.

Brooklyn pulled out a razor and was ready to cut her face open.

Meeka grabbed her friend, shouting, "Brooklyn, come on, let's go!"

"Look at that bitch! Look at her now!" Brooklyn shouted.

Both girls hurried back to the car and sped away, leaving the girl sprawled out on the concrete looking like she'd been hit by a Mack truck.

Meeka knew Brooklyn was more than qualified for the position. The bitch was harder than most niggas she knew. Luca would be pleased.

Brooklyn bragged about the ass-whipping as Meeka hurried away from the area, turning corners hastily and laughing herself.

Meeka had two more people like Brooklyn to look at—two more ruthless young muthafuckas who didn't give a fuck.

***

Chin was a pretty boy with light caramel skin, honey-colored eyes, and silky light brown hair. His mother was Black American and American Indian. Growing up and living on the mean streets of Bed-Stuy, the do-or-die neighborhood, Chin used to get picked on a lot. In grade school, he used to get chased home from school every night, and in junior high school they bullied him. His mother put him in boxing, so he would learn how to defend himself, and over time he became lethal with his hands.

In the eighth grade he started making a name for himself, knocking out the same muthafuckas who once bullied him. But then in high school, things were different. No one fought anymore. They shot or stabbed first.

Soon Chin, because of his pretty boy looks, started packing a pistol and joined a fierce gang called the Bee Boys. It didn't take him long to graduate to murder before dropping out of high school with a tenth-grade education. By the time Chin was eighteen, he had a fierce reputation for violence and murders and a history of many arrests.

Chin's partner in crime was Scotty, a quick-tempered triggerman who loved guns and bloodshed. With no mother or father, he grew up in the ghetto pits of hell, seeing violence and murder from the time he was five years old. He had been sexually abused and bullied, like Chin. Scotty knew about every brand of gun, the calibers, the kill zones, and what kind of damage they were able to do to the body.

Chin and Scotty were a pair of serial killers who'd left their mark of destruction—bodies piled up in blood and bullet holes—from state to state.

Their motivation for killing was money. Like the Joker once said, "If you're good at something, why do it for free?"

Meeka knew them both, having grown up with them in Brooklyn, and she was desperate to recruit them to come work for Luca.

Chapter 12

A week after Luca's talk with Dominic's receptionist she still hadn't received a phone call or any word about her attorney's whereabouts. Upset and rage started to turn into panic and frustration. She wanted to know where he was, but most critically, where the fuck all of her money was. Every day, her fortune was dwindling. She had no product or cash. Supposedly it was all incinerated in the fire. She had real estate, investments, stocks and bonds, and supposedly a strong savings that was arranged by Dominic just in case of rainy days. This was a fuckin' thunderstorm for Luca. She was stupid to actually trust him. In her heart, she knew something was wrong. She felt so foolish.

She called his office repeatedly, but his receptionist answered all the time with the same sad news. From her bedroom, Luca shouted and cursed into the phone, unaware that her grandmother could overhear her.

Her grandmother didn't intervene. She simply went into the living room, sat in her favorite chair, and turned on the television. She remembered the name Luca had screamed out from the bedroom, and having a habit of recording her favorite programs, especially on CNBC, she went looking for it on her long list of recorded shows.

Meanwhile, Luca was reaching a dead end with the bitch on the other end of the phone. She became so heated, she hung up on the dizzy receptionist wanting to put a hit out on the bitch. She believed the woman was lying. It wasn't a secret that Dominic was fucking that bitch.

Luca paced her bedroom, trying to come up with a master plan. This wasn't going to ruin her. She knew Meeka was out there recruiting a team of killers for her to keep a stronghold on her empire. The wolves were knocking at her door thinking she was weak. They were ready to sink their teeth into everything she had worked for. She had to prove them wrong.

Luca stormed out of her room scowling. She went into the living room where her grandmother was seated quietly.

When Luca's grandmother's saw her irate expression, she called out to her. "Luca, come sit with me. I need to show you something."

"I don't have time, Grandma."

"Yes, you do. Come now, and sit." She patted the spot beside her.

Luca, impatience and worry written all over her face, sighed with frustration and sat next to her sickly grandmother. She didn't have time to sit with the old woman and watch some ridiculous TV show. Her life was on the line.

"Who's Dominic?" Lucinda asked.

Luca was surprised at the name coming out of her grandmother's mouth. How did she know? Was she snooping on her conversation?

"He's nobody, Grandma."

"Young woman, don't lie to me. I know he's someone important in your world. I overheard you screaming his name into the cell phone to someone. Now, who is he? And what has this man done to you?"

Luca heaved another strong sigh, locking eyes with her grandmother.

"He's my attorney, Grandma."

"Is his full name Dominic Sirocco?"

Luca found herself dumbfounded by her grandmother's words. *How did she know? What the fuck is going on?* Luca asked herself. "Yes. But how did you know?"

"I just know." Lucinda picked up the remote to the cable box and TV and turned it on. "I need you to watch something, Luca. I recorded it last week."

Luca was puzzled.

Suddenly, the popular show on CNBC called *American Greed* appeared on the small television screen in front of them. Luca didn't have a clue what was going on or why she was watching the show with her grandmother. She wanted to get up. She had too much on her mind to waste time on a couch watching some stupid show on cable.

Lucinda fast-forwarded to a particular segment of the show. Luca unexpectedly found herself flabbergasted at the picture and name on the screen—Dominic Sirocco.

Suddenly, she was interested. Her grandmother didn't say a word, but let the show speak for itself.

Luca's eyes were glued to the TV screen. The fugitive program broadcast that the charismatic attorney was on the run, that he was the subject of a nationwide search for pulling off an elaborate Ponzi scheme, defrauding dozens of his clients out of hundreds of millions.

What the fuck! Luca was stuck on stupid.

Grandmother and granddaughter were glued to the show, which went into detail about his elaborate crimes, from his early beginnings to the present with him on the run. Luca wondered how he went over fifteen years without getting caught yet.

One of Dominic's earlier crimes was embezzling millions of dollars from clients he represented in automobile accidents and other personal injury matters. Without his clients' permission, he would settle cases and forge their signatures on the settlement checks received from insurance companies. He'd also stolen $400,000 from an account set up to benefit the family of a deceased client.

Dominic owned homes worth $7.2 million, some decked out with bowling alleys and $100,000 video arcades. One of his places had a 1950s-style diner, a screening room, and go-cart track out back. He also spent lavishly on gifts for friends and family members, racking up $1 million on his Visa card. He'd also donated $2 million to various charities, owned 9 cars, and spent $1.4 million on jets and vacations. He'd also shelled out

$400,000 on sports tickets, sitting in a luxury box at Jets and Giants football games. He did all this, running a $100-million-dollar Ponzi scheme from his office.

The scheme was simple enough. Dominic had told potential investors of a company, a company he was a part of, that was secure with lucrative contracts with companies including Best Buy, Target, and AT&T, urging them to get in on the action. Dominic guaranteed a ten percent return on investors' money in 30 days and even sent out testimonials that he was the real deal. Prospective investors also received documents that outlined $70 million worth of bogus service contracts.

The scheme lasted ten years, with millions pouring in from top-notch associates, businessmen, and friends.

When the *American Greed* program ended, Luca couldn't believe what she heard. A prominent defense attorney with a faultless acquittal record got greedy and wanted so much more. Her disbelief went from utter shock to bitter rage and anger. He'd taken off with her money, along with dozens of his clients', and he was still out there, probably residing somewhere in the Cayman Islands sipping on martinis.

Chapter 13

World felt like Robert De Niro's character laying eyes on Sharon Stone in *Casino* when he first laid eyes on Maribel. She was extremely beautiful, and her attitude resembled Sharon Stone's character from the movie—vibrant and rough. She was a fierce hustler and sharp like a Samurai sword. From the South Bronx, she was of Puerto Rican descent, her skin an olive brown mixture, and she had wide hips and sensuous eyes, with dark brown, almost-curly hair.

But she was only sixteen.

World first laid eyes on her when he was conducting business in the Bronx. She was storming out of a corner bodega cursing and heated. He happened to be driving by in his black-on-black Benz with the tinted windows when he came across the melee that was about to ensue.

The owner of the store accused Maribel of stealing from him. He confronted her, she got loud, and he got louder. He tried to unzip her frayed bubble coat and remove the items hidden inside, but Maribel wasn't having it. She quickly smacked him and punched him in the face and then hurried out the door.

The man's family didn't take the disrespect lightly. His two daughters and sister came at Maribel as she tried to elude them. The younger sister snatched Maribel by the back of her coat the second she exited the store.

Maribel spun around and got into the daughter's face. "Get the fuck off me, bitch!" she yelled heatedly.

"Fuck you, bitch! You hit my fuckin' father!"

"He a bitch-ass nigga!"

Yelling, pushing, and screaming quickly ensued. Maribel found herself outnumbered by the family, but she refused to back down. World was drawn to the confrontation. Smoking his Black & Mild and smiling, he watched from a short distance, transfixed on the Puerto Rican bombshell.

"I got my bet on shorty," he said to his henchman.

The man laughed.

The second daughter stepped toward Maribel and attempted to unzip her coat to retrieve the stolen items, and shouting, "Give back what you fuckin' stole, you bum bitch!"

But when she tried to place her hands on Maribel, Maribel swung and two-pieced her, and she went down like Frazier going against Ali.

The younger daughter lunged at Maribel and instantly got hit with a hard left, then a wobbling right, and then her long weave became entangled in Maribel's fist with Maribel trying to pull every inch of the girl's weave out of her head.

"Get off me, bitch!" the girl shouted, clearly outmatched.

"I told you don't fuck wit' me, stupid bitch!" Maribel screamed, her foot in the girl's stomach.

The girl folded over from the pain. Maribel fought the two sisters and their aunt in front of the bodega. The crowd cheered. Everyone knew Maribel was a beast on the streets.

World was impressed. The young girl was a woman to his liking. The way she handled herself was outstanding. When the storeowner tried to aid his daughters and sister with subduing Maribel so they could call the police, World saw it as his cue to intervene. He flicked away the Black & Mild and coolly walked over.

The owner snatched Maribel.

World grabbed him, sternly saying, "Get ya fuckin' hands off of her."

The man turned around scowling. But he took one look at World and suddenly turned yellow, like a scared cat.

World lifted his shirt, revealing the 9 mm tucked in his waistband. Suddenly the man didn't want any problems.

"Fuck off, nigga!" World told him.

He and his daughters retreated back into the bodega.

Maribel glared at World. "I can fight my own battles, muthafucka."

World grinned. "I know. I already seen that. Just thought you might need a little help."

Maribel frowned. Her hair was a little disheveled, but she didn't have a scratch or bruise on her. The bonus was, she still had the things she had shoplifted from the bodega.

"You need a ride, shorty?" World asked.

"From you?" Maribel asked with attitude.

"Yeah, from me. You know who the fuck I am?"

Maribel didn't have a clue. She sized up World and assumed he was someone who thought he was important—definitely a hustler with his bling shining like a rap star, and his goon standing behind him looking like a killer.

"Who are you?" she asked.

World chuckled at her nonchalant reply. He glanced at his goon. "You believe shorty?"

The goon smiled. They thought she was cute. She had World's eye and his undivided attention.

"My name's World. What's yours, shorty? Or did ya mama warn you not to talk to strangers?"

"Fuck my mama and fuck you! You don't know me."

World could only chuckle at the disrespectful and immature comment thrown at him. If it was anyone else, they would have been murdered. "Damn, she's feisty."

"She is."

"I like that."

Maribel was a firecracker, always ready to go off. If she was playing hard to get, then World was feeding into it.

"Look, I'm being a gentleman, shorty. Let me give you a ride somewhere. I ain't gonna bite. Let's you and me talk, I like ya style."

Maribel threw her hand on her hip and shifted her weight onto one leg. The look she gave World was a cold one. She thought about it briefly and made up her mind. "Fuck it. Let's ride then, nigga. I'm down."

She followed World to his Benz and climbed into the backseat behind him. Once she was settled in, she finally unzipped her frayed bubble coat and started removing a few of her stolen items: a box of cereal, a loaf of bread, and cookies. She dumped everything on the seat next to her.

"Damn, shorty! You that hungry?" World joked.

Maribel shot him a disapproving stare. "Don't fuckin' judge me. My family ain't rich like you, so I do what I gotta do to survive."

"Nah, shorty I ain't judging you. I understand. I been there myself too."

Maribel continually frowned.

"What's ya name?"

She glared at him and then said, "Maribel."

"I like that. How old are you?"

"Sixteen."

"Sixteen," he said, smiling and nodding. "I can deal wit' that."

"Deal wit' what, nigga?" Maribel snapped back.

World didn't answer her. Her look told him she was poor, from the streets, and desperate for food and cash. Her clothing was worn out, and her sneakers looked older than her. But behind the poverty and ghetto attitude, she was beautiful. He reached into his pocket and pulled out a wad of hundred-dollar bills. He showed off ten thousand dollars in his hands. It was more money than she had seen in her lifetime.

"I'm gonna do you a favor, shorty," World said, peeling off hundred after hundred from his large wad.

Maribel became wide-eyed at the cash in front of her. She felt her mouth watering, anxious to get her hands on that kind of money. She and her family had been poor and underprivileged for a very long time.

World handed her five hundred dollars, saying, "Here, shorty, that's fo' you and ya peoples, so y'all won't go hungry tonight."

At first, Maribel looked hesitant about taking the money. "And what I gotta do for it?" she asked with a raised eyebrow.

"You ain't gotta do nothin' shorty. I'm just givin' it to you."

World put the money into her hands. She didn't resist it. Having five hundred dollars was a much-needed blessing. It felt like gold in her hands.

"I just wanna see you again," World said.

"I'm sixteen."

"And?" replied World.

He was twenty-nine, thirteen years her senior, and wasn't afraid of any statutory rape charges if he got with Maribel. He was a king that got whatever he wanted. He wanted the young girl to become his, feeling it was love at first sight.

Maribel folded the money in her hand.

World uttered out, "I lied. There is a catch."

She frowned. "Fuck you! I ain't a fuckin' prostitute!"

"Nah, the catch is, I just wanna see you again, and I want you to become my bitch."

"What?"

"I can take care of you."

Hearing the sound of that was like music to her ears. Maribel grew up hard, learning how to take care of herself. Her family was considered ghetto trash. She grew up fighting, selling drugs, and shoplifting to make ends meet and help support her family. World talked to her like he could become her Santa Claus. But he wanted sex too—they always wanted sex. Maribel wasn't a stranger to sex, spreading her legs to get what she needed.

She locked eyes with him. "You wanna take care of me," she returned with incredulity in her tone.

"I got you, shorty. Whatever you need, it's yours."

"Whatever I need, huh?"

He nodded.

In fact, she needed a favor.

The Benz came to a stop in front of the towering housing projects on Randall Avenue. She looked out the window and noticed Tyrone, her ex-boyfriend, exiting the lobby and walking their way. Lately, she had a beef with him. He stole from her when she only had little, fucked her best friend, and talked shit about her and her family. He was a well-known drug dealer on the block, somewhat feared and noted to be fuckin' crazy. He only used Maribel for sex and as a drug mule. He underpaid her, abused her, and taunted her by being with her friends and other bitches from her building. Maribel was sick of his shit. She wanted payback.

She pointed in Tyrone's direction and explained her situation to World. "I want him fucked up."

World didn't hesitate to take care of the problem. He said to his goon behind the wheel, "Mark, go handle that fo' shorty."

Mark nodded and climbed out of the car with a Glock gripped in his hand. He nonchalantly walked toward Tyrone's direction, and when he got close to the young hoodlum, he lunged at him and started to pistol-whip him on the sidewalk. Tyrone went down, his skull split open by the brutal assault abruptly executed on him. Mark was all over the boy like bees on honey. The assault was rapid and vicious.

When Mark was done pulverizing Tyrone into the pavement, he calmly walked away and got back into the Benz, acting like nothing happened.

Maribel was impressed. "Damn!"

"Did that get your attention?" World asked.

She nodded.

"So, I'm gonna see you again?" he asked.

Maribel smiled.

"Yeah, you can see me again." She gave him her number.

Maribel got out the car feeling like she was that bitch. She passed Tyrone sprawled across the concrete passed out and bleeding.

By this time, a small crowd had gathered around him, shocked that he had been assaulted.

Maribel went into her building with World watching her from the backseat of the Benz. He lit another cigarette and said to Mark, "Yeah, that's gonna be my prized bitch, Mark. Lovin' shorty already."

Mark nodded and smiled.

***

Maribel walked into the cramped three-bedroom apartment she shared with her fat mother, Rebecca, who was thirty-two, her drunk father Jeffery, thirty, her two uncles, one aunt, and cousins. They lived third world in their project apartment. She looked around her cluttered home and sighed deeply. She couldn't live like this anymore. She didn't show her family the five hundred dollars. Once they got a sniff of money, especially that much, they would become like piranhas smelling blood in the water. They would come swarming at her, hungry for a taste.

She decided to keep the money a secret from them. It was hers to spend, and if she felt charitable, then she would trickle a little off to them.

***

Within weeks, World and Maribel became an item. He started tricking on her whole ghetto family, raining thousands of dollars on them like it was nothing, buying Maribel whatever she needed or wanted—clothes, jewelry, a car when she didn't even have her license, large amounts of money in her pockets, and the respect of being his woman.

In return, she gave World some of the best pussy he'd ever had. She was young, tight, and her pussy perpetually wet. She sucked his dick like she was legal. She became devoted to him. He took care of her, and she took care of him.

Her family didn't care about the age difference. They treated World like he was royalty. His money made them love him, and they also could care less that he was a murderous and sadistic drug dealer. In fact, the men in the family wanted World to put on to his drug crew. When he went over to their ghetto apartment, Maribel's mother was all smiles, her father was kissing his ass, and her uncles tried to impress him.

Rebecca was constantly meddling in her daughter's business. Whenever she got the chance, she would pull her daughter into the bedroom to talk. "He's a good man, Maribel. I like him. So don't you fuck this up for us. You hear me? He's good to us."

Maribel smirked, locking eyes with her mother.

"Yes, I know. He's good to me," she uttered with her ghetto attitude. "He's my man. And y'all got y'all nice things because of me and my pussy. I got that nigga sprung, Ma, so don't you forget that."

"Bitch, don't let it go to ya head," Rebecca said.

"You don't let it go to yours either."

Rebecca frowned at her daughter.

Maribel knew her mother had eyes for World. She proclaimed to love their father, but made it a habit to fuck younger men, tempting them with some cougar pussy and old-school head.

"All I'm sayin' to you, Maribel is, just make it last," Rebecca advised her second oldest child.

"Believe me, Ma, I ain't fuckin' this one up. Me and my man don't play. He got shit on lock, and he gonna be around to stay. Ain't nobody taking my boo down, 'cuz he got it like that. That nigga is Superman."

"I hope ya right," Rebecca replied, warily.

Chapter 14

The dark-colored Yukon crossed the Verrazano Bridge into Brooklyn and merged onto the Gowanus Expressway, heading north toward Harlem. Soon the Yukon arrived in Manhattan, doing sixty miles per hour on the FDR. Once in Harlem, it parked on Second Avenue, across from the Wagner Houses. With spring almost right around the corner, the weather was breaking, and the city was seeing nicer days. The people were outside enjoying the weather, and traffic was everywhere. It was good to be home.

Unbeknownst to the hood, Squirrel had just arrived back in town. He gazed at his former territory from the backseat of the Yukon and frowned. World had pushed him out and embarrassed him. Now he was back with a thorough crew of soldiers and a quality product, hell-bent on taking back what was once his.

Three goons accompanied him in the Yukon. In the back of the truck sat several AR-15s and a small arsenal ready for a war. For the past two months, Squirrel had been in Charlotte, North Carolina, remaining low key as he came up with a master plan. He linked up with his cousin, Homando, an ex-Marine who was dishonorably discharged for sexual assault against a female Marine and drug use. He was convicted at a general court-martial for his offenses, and lost all his benefits as a veteran.

Once home, Homando used his skills on the streets to become a gun-for-hire for drug dealers. He soon got with other dishonorably discharged Marines with nothing to lose, and they formed a deadly crew, taking over the drug trade in Charlotte and becoming contractors for murder.

When Squirrel and Homando reunited, Squirrel expressed his pain to his first cousin. Homando made it known to him they were family, but he didn't come cheap. Squirrel was ready to extract his revenge, and World and Luca were at the top of his list.

He had gotten back with his baby mama Angel, and she held him down while he was hiding out from the Colombians.

Then he stalked Luca. He and his cousin needed a windfall, so he went to Luca's home, found her cash and her drugs, took everything, and then burned her house down to the ground. For a moment, he'd sat parked some distance from the fire and watched the bitch's home become engulfed in flames, smoke billowing as far as the eye could see. It was minor payback. He hooked his cousin up with the product, and then he was able to make his situation right with the Colombians, getting back into their good graces.

Squirrel moved weight with his cousin in North Carolina for a while until he got his paper back up and recruited his cousin's insane crew as an army of contract killers. They were all military trained, highly skilled with weapons, bomb making, surveillance, and killing. To go against World, he knew he needed an insane team that didn't give a fuck. They'd all seen their fair share of bloodshed, war, and death while touring overseas in Baghdad and Afghanistan.

Squirrel lingered on Second Avenue for a moment. He missed home. The 20 BLOCC and Flow Boyz were out on the streets making their presence known, as was law enforcement. Since that bloody shootout between his men and World's goons, the NYPD had placed a mobile police station with a watchtower on the corner of Second Avenue and 124th Street.

Squirrel smoked a cigarette, observing everything.

"This is it," he told the men in the Yukon. "This is home."

They remained quiet, looking around, watching the block, eager to cause havoc in Harlem. Squirrel was paying them a small fortune and promising them a nice percentage of a lucrative area if they got rid of World.

Squirrel's crew had strong ties with a notorious gang known in Charlotte as the Hidden Valley Kings, HVK for short, formed in the late 1980s by a former Vice Lords member from Chicago. They represented themselves with black bandannas.

Homando was once a gun-for-hire for the gang, implementing the military tactics he'd learned in the service on the streets. He made his way up the ranks and executed a hostile takeover.

"Let's go," Squirrel told the driver. He had another destination he wanted to check out.

They made their way farther uptown, toward 155th Street. Every part of Harlem was alive and pulsating with movement, from block to block. Traffic swamped the streets. Everywhere and anywhere, money was being made, legal and illegal. From 110th Street to Washington Heights, uptown was a goldmine, and the players didn't want to leave the playground.

"Make a right here," Squirrel told the driver.

The Yukon moved through the iron-clad borough easily, its North Carolina plate standing out. The truck made a second right and then a left and finally came to a stop in front of a five-story walk-up near Riverside Drive. The two-way street they parked on was wide with traffic flowing on the fading day. The building Squirrel scoped out was old and standard, the lobby nestled away from the street with a wide pathway.

"This is it," Squirrel let the men know.

They waited, their hearts stuck on mayhem. They watched every square inch of the place, itching for some action. They collected the AR-15 from the back and locked and loaded. Squirrel's intel had told him the scheduled pickup was seven p.m., in another half hour.

"We wait," Squirrel told the killers in the Yukon.

More time went by with Squirrel watching people coming and going from the building. His ultimate weapon was the element of surprise.

At seven p.m., on cue, a white Lincoln Navigator parked in front of the building, and two of World's henchmen men stepped out to collect payment. They strolled into the five-story walk-up like routine.

"I want y'all to fuck these niggas up," Squirrel said.

Ski masks pulled over their heads, each man gripped an AR-15, 223-caliber, magazine-fed. In a few short moments, they were about to run the sidewalk red with blood.

Ten minutes later, the same two men started to exit the building carrying a small black bag.

"It's play time, niggas," Squirrel said. "Let's do this shit."

The doors to the Yukon flew open, and the goons quickly made their way out, machine guns itching to scream out. Three masked gunmen, including Squirrel, went for the two men carrying the bag, and the fourth went gunning for the driver behind the wheel of the Navigator.

Abruptly, the ex-Marines-turned-rogue savagely opened fire on the two henchmen, spraying their bodies with bullets and dropping them dead on the concrete. The sound of the AR-15s echoed loudly in the surrounding area.

The driver heard the sound of gunfire, but before he could react, glass shattered around him, and his blood sprayed the front seat.

Squirrel enjoyed it. This was his payback.

"Knock, knock, muthafuckas," Squirrel said through clenched teeth. "I'm fuckin' home."

He snatched a hundred thousand in cash from their bloody hands before hurrying away from the crime scene. He was ready to take back what was once his, reclaim the throne, and become the king of Harlem again.

Chapter 15

The Commission consisted of twelve men—corrupt police officers, detectives, lieutenants, and captains—with a stranglehold on the streets of New York City. They were all smart, powerful, and highly dangerous. They hadn't gotten their power by being weak, stupid, or careless. The board sat around a circular, mahogany table as if they were chiefs of a Fortune 500 company discussing their latest merger. These men had only one agenda—making as much money possible and killing whoever got in their way.

They were discussing a pair of cousins, Luca and World. Folders were passed out with headshots, addresses, and hangout spots. Each man was smirking at the potential problem.

"He's become more of a liability to us than an asset," Captain Clark said, staring at World's ugly mug shot.

"I agree," Lieutenant Greenwood chimed.

"That shooting in Harlem two days ago, when three of his men were gunned down making a pickup? Media is all over that. And I'm hearing Squirrel is back in town. They said it was his doing," a detective said.

Lieutenant Davis added, "World fucked up. He should have gotten rid of Squirrel when he had the chance. Instead, the stupid nigger wants to play games with other niggers. We should let the niggers kill the niggers. I don't give a fuck."

"We don't need to attract the media's attention and have them snooping around. A war in Harlem, that kind of violence and bloodshed, it's bad for business."

"I agree," Captain Anderson said.

Every man in the room had ten or more years on the police force and operated out of a range of precincts throughout the city—the Bronx, Queens, Brooklyn, Harlem, Staten Island, and Manhattan. They became killers and drug dealers with badges, seeing how profitable it was being on the other side of the law, playing both sides of the fence, and hiding their illegal activities behind the NYPD. They shook down drug dealers, extorted drug crews and business, and also became the eyes and ears of fierce drug crews, letting them know of future indictments, snitches in their camps, and giving out the 411 on who was who in the game.

Xavier was sitting at the helm of the table listening to everyone speak. He understood their worries. They had to take a vote around the room to see who would live and who would die. Most of the men in the room felt the meeting was biased. The majority of the Commission knew the outcome, and most didn't fully comprehend why they had to go through such shenanigans for a lowlife thug named World.

Xavier wanted order and a structure so tight and unbreakable, not even the mayor of New York could penetrate it. With millions of dollars from drugs and killings, they were able to buy off or bribe anyone in the city or buy anything. They had power and respect, and they had influential people in high places supporting them—judges, politicians, businessmen, and even the Mafia.

The Commission gazed at Xavier. It was his call. He'd brought World into their hands; now they wanted him gone.

"He's a fuckin' thug, Xavier," Captain Clark said.

"More like a lunatic." Detective Holden shook his head. "He's gonna tear this city apart looking for Squirrel wanting payback. It's best to put out the fire before it spreads."

"World isn't a businessman. He's a savage. He's stupid. And his bitch cousin is a problem. From my understanding, she's blackmailing and extorting some of our people with videos and pictures of them in compromising and incriminating situations," Sergeant Ripple said.

Xavier shrugged. "She's a smart girl."

"She needs to be smart and dead," Detective Holden said.

"The fact is, Xavier, World doesn't do as we say. He's a loose cannon out there," Lieutenant Greenwood stated. "Jesus, he cut off the head of Big Show's son and left it on the bed for him to find."

"Psychotic muthafucka!" Sergeant Ripple yapped out.

"And isn't he fuckin' a sixteen-year-old girl?"

"Stupid mothafucker!"

Xavier heard their gripes. They wanted World dead, but he saw a better plan. He stood up casually and looked into the worried faces of all the men seated around the table. World was dangerous and could easily come gunning for them and their families as they were gunning for him.

"I hear your qualms," Xavier said. "I understand World's a liability, but he also made us a lot of money. He's killed for us, yes, but he doesn't even know that most of you exist. He knows about the Commission, but not the faces. He's seen my face, but he doesn't know my position."

"Where are you going with this, Xavier?"

"What I'm telling you is, everybody wants someone dead. Understood. But let us wait. Play this game like chess, not checkers, and allow Squirrel to murder Luca, and eventually, someone will slip. Most likely it'll be Squirrel, a World kills him for us like previously planned. Then we take World down, arrest him, and have him killed in jail quietly. Kill three birds with one stone."

They thought about it. It seemed like a good plan. They had contract killers in the prison system, and a shank thrust into World's chest meant no murder investigation on the streets, but an expected death inside jail.

Xavier didn't want World killed yet. He had something else sinister planned for him. He was a headache, but he was an effective killing machine. Unbeknownst to the Commission, Xavier was ready to put World's deadly skills to use for his own benefit.

Chapter 16

World rode shotgun in the Pathfinder with his goons, a Glock on his lap. K'wan was behind the wheel, the sawed-off shotgun between his legs. He had become one of the deadliest killers in World's crew. He and his brother were indisputably proving themselves, laying muthafuckas down and spraying blood all around. They were riding around Harlem, looking for Squirrel.

When World got word that three of his men were gunned down like dogs, he didn't flip out. He kept his cool. It was all part of the game. He could care less that Squirrel was back in town and trying to make some noise. World looked at Squirrel as an insect, a nasty little bug that was about to get squashed under his boot. In his mind, Squirrel was still a lightweight, no matter how many soldiers and artillery he'd brought back with him.

World smiled at the thought of Squirrel being back home. At first he was upset that Squirrel had tried to kill Luca. Now he looked at it as a plus. Squirrel could try again and kill his cousin. It was something he himself couldn't do.

He loved tormenting her, fucking with her mind, taking from her, and destroying the world around her.

Another benefit of having Squirrel back in town was, he could rob that nigga again. His Bad Boy product was running low. His relationship with Xavier was rocky, and Harlem was thirsty for some quality dope and coke. He had his scouts out on the streets looking for crews to rob and kill. If any of his scouts sniffed out quality product, World was taking it by force.

World was going through money it like it was water. He had an army of soldiers who needed to get paid. He also had a fly bitch he kept in Gucci and Prada.

It was no secret that everyone feared World. And it was no secret that he and his bitch were becoming the Bonnie and Clyde of the city, and Maribel was just as crazy, possessive, and jealous as he was.

As World drove around Harlem with his crew, his mind drifted to the incident that had happened a few days earlier. He even smiled at the thought of it.

***

One of Maribel's young friends caught World's eye. He liked what he saw. She was five-foot-six, petite and athletic, with dyed blonde hair, hazel eyes, and pouty lips. She made eye contact with him and smiled. That was all it took. World made conversation with the seventeen-year-old and disappeared with her to receive some oral pleasure.

They concealed themselves in the narrow stairway. World forced the girl down on her knees, and she hurriedly undid his jeans to whip out his dick. He leaned against the wall with her in the kneeling position, and she gently took him into her mouth, sucking his dick like a two-dollar whore in the project stairway. He fucked her mouth while she stroked his balls in her hand. She was sucking it like there was a prize in the center of his dick. He grabbed her hair and slammed his balls against her chin, feeling the wetness of her mouth. World was in oral bliss with the girl's talented mouth sucking him off.

But then, suddenly, the doorway to the stairwell slammed open, and Maribel, a sharp razor in her hand, came charging in, lunging for her friend. She attacked her friend, repeatedly slicing her across the face with the razor, and the skin on her face opened up like a zipper.

"Fuckin' bitch! Don't fuck wit' my man, you fuckin' slut!" she shouted.

By the time World and his men restrained her, the poor girl's face looked like a jigsaw puzzle coated with blood.

World didn't have a choice. He looked at his henchman and said, "Take care of her," meaning, kill her and discard her body.

They carried her out while World and his bitch argued in the stairway. Maribel wanted to cut World too, but she wasn't *that* stupid.

***

As World drove around Harlem with his goons searching for Squirrel, his phone rang. He looked at the caller ID, and saw it was an unknown caller. He answered.

The male voice on the other end was calm and demanding. "You get a reprieve, for now," he told World.

"What?"

"We took a vote, and for now you're still some good use to us," Xavier said. "I looked out for you."

World chuckled at his comment, not taking it seriously. "And that's supposed to be some concern to me?"

"Listen, you ignorant fuck, you think you're fuckin' invincible, World? Anybody can be touched."

"Exactly."

"I warned you; don't bite the hand that feeds you."

"I'm pretty capable of feeding myself, Xavier," World responded. "Why the fuck you callin' me?"

For weeks, things between World and Xavier had been tense. They'd had a few choice words for each other. They tolerated each other because each one had something the other wanted. World needed his supply, and Xavier needed his insanity.

World and his crew weren't scared to do anything, even killing a federal judge in his own courtroom. They were just that crazy to pull it off, for the right price.

"We need to meet," Xavier said.

"When and where?"

"I'll call you back with the details. Meanwhile, keep yourself alive, you stupid fuck!" Xavier hung up.

World smirked. He was never worried about death. In his mind, he was the Grim Reaper. Everybody feared him, and in his warped mind, even the Commission feared him too. It was the only reason they wanted him dead, and why

Xavier continued to play somewhat nice. He'd heard of the Commission a few times. He knew they were corrupt, wicked cops, but he wasn't afraid to go against them.

They drove around for hours, but there was no sign of Squirrel. No one knew where he was. No one was talking. Squirrel was playing it smart, hiding out, probably not in Harlem. New York was a big city to search. World had his killers spread out in Brooklyn, Queens, and as far as Long Island. The minute Squirrel popped his head out of the small hole he was hiding in, World was ready to take it off, but not before having some fun with his prey first.

World's cell phone rang again. This time he was caught completely off guard. The person had some nerves, some balls on her for a bitch. It was Luca calling out the blue. *Did she call to surrender herself?* The thought put a wicked smile on his face.

He answered her call and casually said, "Hey, cuz. How you been? I missed you."

Chapter 17

The Dominic scandal was like the straw that broke the camel's back. For several days, Luca locked herself into her small bedroom, feeling angry and embarrassed. She felt played and used, with enemies coming against her from every direction. She had hit rock bottom. She was back living in the ghetto with barely any money.

Sometimes, she would peer out the window in a daze for hours, watching the activities of the ghetto from sunup to sundown, and there were times where she felt despondent and suicidal. Her money and drugs had burned to ashes, and she didn't have a connect. Her attorney had scammed her out of all her investment money right under her nose. She didn't have Clyde in her life. Her best friend Phaedra had turned against her and was out there somewhere, maybe plotting her murder. She'd also heard through the grapevine that Squirrel was back in town and hitting hard. And with her own family against her, how could she win?

Luca didn't want to cry, but she did, feeling trapped in hopelessness. She didn't have love in her life. She didn't have trust anywhere. The only thing she felt could bring her some semblance of peace was seeing Dominic Sirocco and The Kabakoff brothers in their graves.

The nightmares were returning. Naomi was haunting her again. Luca could feel the bitch's malevolent spirit surrounding her, her voice taunting her like fingernails scraping against a chalkboard. At night, when she tried to get some sleep, the room would become darker, and sudden chills would come over her. It felt like a violent force encircled her and wanted to pull her into the darkness.

Naomi, back from the grave with a smirk on her face, was lurking in Luca's mind, haunting her. "You killed me, and this is payback. Payback, bitch!" Naomi's ghastly voice cried out in Luca's ear.

Luca tried not to panic.

"You'll never survive without me," she taunted. Her laughter in Luca's ear was sinister and chilling.

Luca would twist and turn in her bed. Sometimes she would wake up screaming in the middle of the night. She could feel Naomi trying to drag her into hell. She could feel sharp teeth gnawing at her ankles, monstrous hands pulling her into the dark depths of sorrow. Luca tried to resist, but this wicked force was relentless and strong.

"I knew you would fail. Look at you! Look at you!" she heard Naomi's voice chant.

Luca refused to give Naomi the satisfaction of seeing her lose. She had come too far to give up. She closed her eyes, clenched her fists, and screamed at the top of her lungs. "Leave me alone! Leave me the fuck alone! You're dead! I killed you!" Her voice echoed throughout the apartment, even waking up her grandmother and startling the old woman.

Luca screamed again loudly with every breath in her body. She glared at Naomi's transparent soul and wanted to kill the bitch again. She fought the pain surging through her, trying to snatch away her sanity. She fought it until it was gone.

She jumped out of her bed, her breath sparse. She was gasping for air.

Her grandmother knocked on her door. "Luca, is everything okay in there?"

Luca felt like her chest was tightening, and her heart beat rapidly.

Her grandmother continued knocking at the door.

"I'm okay, Grandma," Luca answered.

"Why did you scream?"

"I just had a bad dream."

"We all do sometimes," her grandmother said.

Luca walked toward her bedroom window and peered out at the dark. It was three a.m., and the ghetto was quiet. She continued taking deep breaths, cooling down her nerves.

That night she devised a plan. She knew how to talk and negotiate business. It was time to put her gift of gab to use. It was time to do her own liquidation of all the valuable assets she had left.

✳✳✳

She took a trip back north to Rockaway Park to retrieve and sell the Audi. Luca also had to sell a few other items she had brought to her grandmother's before the fire like her jewelry and mink coat. It was time to get back on the map. She made $120,000. She needed to buy her way out of a complex and hazardous situation. It was time to get some allies, even if she had to pay for them. Luca felt she had nothing to lose. There were too many enemies facing her everywhere she turned.

With a bag filled with cash and a shovel to dig her way out of trouble, Luca turned to her grandmother for help, with her grandmother sitting in her favorite place in the apartment—at the kitchen table peering out the window at the activity below her.

Luca sat opposite Lucinda. "Grandma, I'm in trouble. I need help."

Lucinda sighed heavily and locked eyes with her beautiful granddaughter. "Is it drugs?"

"It's so many things, Grandma."

Her grandma was ready to listen intently. It wouldn't be the first time someone in their family got into serious trouble, and she had already heard the stories about her granddaughter's wild ways.

Luca started with, "I went to see my father in Clinton."

Her grandmother was shocked to hear that. Travis had been gone from her family's life for so long, when they spoke of him, he sounded like some kind of urban legend.

"And how is he doing?" Lucinda didn't care for the man at all. She just thought it was polite to ask.

"He's doing fine."

Luca went on to say what she and her father talked about. She just needed someone to talk to, someone to listen, and her grandmother was a great listener and advisor.

Luca told Lucinda everything. She felt it was the right thing to do. She went into detail—how it all started, from Nate's death to the drugs. When she talked about the murders and the violence, she swallowed hard, eyeing her grandmother nervously.

Lucinda had become a Christian, but the way she looked at her granddaughter, her eyes wondered who this woman in her home was. The things Luca confessed to were far worse than anything she had heard from anyone. Lucinda already had an idea about Luca selling drugs, but she didn't know the extent of it.

When the conversation had started, Luca was holding her grandmother's hand across the table, but the deeper her talk got, the more she felt her grandmother's grip loosen, like she was pulling away from evil.

"I'm not evil, Grandma."

"The things you are telling me are blasphemous, Luca. How could you do these things? And why? Your grandfather would be spinning in his grave if he heard about you," Lucinda stated, contempt in her voice.

"I had to survive, Grandma."

"Survive? The things you confessed to doing, that's not surviving. It's appalling and wicked."

"I'm sorry, Grandma. I just wanted to be honest with you."

Lucinda gazed at her granddaughter. She loved Luca greatly, but her confession was making her sick to her stomach. "I'm tempted to kick you out of this home, Luca. I can't have that kind of sin staying with me."

"I understand," Luca replied sadly.

"However, you are my granddaughter, and I love you dearly. But today, your past, your sins, it stops now. I don't want you drug dealing, hanging out. I don't want any violence from you. I'm willing to forgive you, because it's the Christian thing to do. But you get back in school, and you pray to the Lord. I put you in God's hands, because it is only He who can fix you." Lucinda gave Luca an intense stare. "Do you understand me?"

Luca nodded.

"I'm glad you were honest with me. But you broke my heart, Luca. I'm so disappointed with you. You are so much better than this, so much better. You went against everything your grandfather stood for."

Luca's heart fell to the pit of her stomach. Seeing her grandmother upset and hurt was worse than taking a bullet to the chest. She loved that woman. When Luca was down and out, her grandmother was always there for her. When she needed someone to talk to, her grandmother always made time for her. When she needed money or just a hug, it came from her grandmother.

"Promise me today you're done with that life, because, if you're not, you can't stay here. You understand me?"

"I promise, Grandma. I'm done with it."

It was a promise Luca knew she wouldn't be able to keep. She needed her grandmother to do her one more favor.

Luca pulled out her cell phone and placed it on the table. She sighed and said, "I need you to call World for me, because I need to make things right with him, Grandma. We had a falling out, and we need to talk. It is part of my changing."

Lucinda looked skeptical at first. Her grandson World, ever since he was a child, had been a walking nightmare, always getting into bad things and running around the ghetto like he was some demon spawn. Lucinda loved all her grandchildren, but World, since he was born, always had issues with schizophrenia and violence.

"That boy ain't never been right, Luca."

"I know, Grandma, but I need to make it right with him."

Lucinda agreed to call World. Luca knew that there wasn't any way he would try something, or make an attempt on her life, in front of their grandmother. She was taking a huge risk, though, because he was unpredictable.

Lucinda picked up Luca's phone and dialed World. She hadn't spoken to him in months, but she still remembered his number. She spoke to her grandson for a short moment and then handed the phone to Luca.

Luca felt uneasy getting on the phone with him, but it was something she needed to do.

***

The next day World came knocking at his grandmother's door. He had an army lingering outside just in case it was a setup. K'wan, his hard glare aimed at Luca, stood behind World. He had the gun in his waist and was itching to blast anyone that came at them.

When Luca came face to face with her cousin, her heart was about to beat out of her chest. She felt like she was meeting evil in the flesh. He was tall and handsome, but his eyes spoke a level of craziness, that if his look was an earthquake, it would've registered a 9.5 on the Richter scale. He was draped in bling and a leather jacket. It was obvious he was strapped and ready to talk.

Luca took a chance stepping into the hallway alone with him. Her grandmother was sleeping in the bedroom. She didn't want to bring any trouble into her home. He was crazy enough to shoot her dead in the hallway, but World had never disrespected their grandmother's home.

"I'm here, cuz. How's Grandma doing?"

"She's 'sleep," Luca said.

"We should just shoot this fuckin' bitch," K'wan said.

"Chill, nigga. She still family."

K'wan frowned.

Luca held the bag with a hundred thousand large inside of it. She locked eyes with World and said, "We need to talk, just you and me."

"I'm ready."

"Not here. On the roof, alone," she suggested.

World nodded. They walked into the stairway and headed toward the rooftop, just the two of them. Luca kept her pistol close, as did World.

They reached the rooftop. It was a clear, chilly night.

Luca walked toward the edge and gazed over. It was a long drop. World stood closely behind her. She suddenly became nervous.

She took a few steps away from him and the ledge and tossed him the black bag with the one hundred thousand inside. She had decided to keep twenty large for herself.

World looked at the bag. He was confused.

"I want this beef to end between us, World," she said.

World was curious about the bag in his hand. He looked at Luca and asked facetiously, "You got a bomb in here? You planning to blow us both up?"

"No, no bomb. In there is a hundred thousand. The money is yours."

"Mine?" World was shocked by the generous offer. "A hundred thousand cash?"

"Yes."

He smiled. "On what condition, cuz? Because don't shit come free in this world—unless I take it from a muthafucka."

"The money is in exchange for my life," Luca said.

World quickly snatched the pistol from his waistband and pointed it at Luca's head. "You mean the life I can easily take right now?"

Luca didn't budge or cringe. Even though she felt her heart slammed into her throat, she locked eyes with World and coolly said, "I'm sorry for everything. The way I treated you, I disrespected you, World, and I deserve to die."

"You fuckin' right 'bout that."

Luca didn't take her eyes off him and the gun. She swallowed hard. "I should have paid you. I was wrong. I was emotional and out of control."

World stepped closer with his arm outstretched, gun still at the end of it, Luca staring down the barrel. "You damn right, you was out of fuckin' control. I made you. I created you, cuz, and you let it go to ya fuckin' head. Now the Bad Girl queen is down on her luck, and you find yourself crawling back to fuckin' family. Family was the one that started you, bitch, and it will be family that ends you."

He was right. If it wasn't for World, the throne wouldn't have been hers. Nate's death had opened the gates to her wealth and power. She had learned from him, but World gave her the head start.

"You can end me, World. You have the right. You knocked down the queen— checkmate on the board. Or we can talk business, come together, and kill the king."

"And who is the king?"

"Anyone coming against us."

World smirked. "I always wanted to know how to play chess. It looks like a fun game. Can you teach me, cuz?"

What the fuck? Luca thought. *Is this all a joke to him?*

"You was always my favorite cousin, Luca. You stayed to yourself and was very smart. I envied you. I killed Nate because you family, but I wanted my payday too." He lowered the gun from her head.

World only wanted her to acknowledge that if it wasn't for him, then there would be no her. And now that she had somewhat begged for his forgiveness, he was ready for bygones to be bygones. She was still family, and it was hard to kill a cousin who was once close to him.

The two of them had a lengthy talk on the rooftop.

Luca cooled his anger, promising to extend his power and wealth. She made it clear to him that she was a benefit to him alive, not dead.

"With me by your side, World, brains and brawn, we can take over this city and destroy all of our enemies with one swing of the sword."

World smiled. He liked what he was hearing. "The prodigal bitch," he joked. He picked up the bag with the money and placed it under his arm.

Luca felt relieved that she had settled their dispute, but secretly, she was pissed that he had the audacity to take the cash. Although the cash was a peace offering, it was only a fake treaty in her eyes. She had mastered the art of deception and manipulation, and peace with World bought her more time to rebuild.

Chapter 18

World was on top of his game. He was getting good pussy, and he had money to burn and power to wield. He had New York by the balls and was squeezing tight. With Luca's 100k, he decided to treat Maribel and her family to a shopping spree and a night out on the town.

Early that afternoon, the mother, father, sisters and brothers, cousins and other extended family received expensive jewelry from World—big-face diamond watches for the men and diamond tennis bracelets for the ladies.

He took Maribel on a twenty-thousand dollar shopping spree for clothes, shoes, jewelry, manicure, and pedicure, and by the end of the day, he bought her a brand-new car, a fully loaded red convertible BMW 650i with chrome rims. She still didn't have her license, but she was already driving around in an $85,000 car that he had to dig in his own stash to purchase.

Later in the evening, he took the family out to eat at a posh restaurant in the city. Tipping the maître d' $300, the ghetto family received the best table in the place. World was paying for ten family members, and he had his goons eating hearty too. Maribel and her family stood out in the restaurant like Malcolm X at a Klan rally. They were loud, ghetto, and vulgar with their language.

Maribel's father shouted at the waiter serving them, "Yo, papi, where the Cristal at?"

"Damn!" a cousin said. "This joint is nice. I know they got lobster in this bitch."

"Fuck lobster! Get me some Spanish food up in this bitch. A vato hungry than a muthafucka," an uncle said.

Waiters brought out a dozen bottles of pricey champagne, Moët, Dom Pérignon, and Cristal, and what seemed like endless appetizers. Maribel's family ordered everything on the menu, steadily increasing the bill— lobster, shrimp, steaks, oysters, salads, pastas, and more. They ate like royalty, but their table manners were sorely lacking, as they were chewing with their mouths open and drinking champagne from the bottle.

A few patrons in the restaurant decided to make an early exit, disgusted by what they were seeing.

A cousin stood up with a bottle of Moët in his hand. He took a swig from it and raised it toward World. He was tipsy, smiling a drunk smile at World, and gave a toast. "To my nigga World, the true don of fuckin' Harlem. Ain't nobody fuckin' wit' you, my homie. And if they fuck wit' you, then they fuckin' wit' all of us, 'cuz we all family and we all got ya back. You feel me, homes?"

World smiled. He lifted his glass and nodded.

Maribel was all smiles too. She sat close to him and felt like she belonged at his side. She moved her hand underneath the table and subtly started to fondle World's crotch as everyone ate and drank. She unzipped his pants and, on the sly, pulled out his dick and started stroking him.

World could only sit back and enjoy the hand job under the table. He downed champagne as Maribel's manicured fist slid up and down his hardening penis.

She leaned into his ear and whispered, "I fuckin' love you so much, baby."

"I love you too," World replied.

As World ate, she jerked him off, holding his dick firmly. He kept his cool though, enjoying the sensation.

Maribel's mother, Rebecca, eyed them both from across the table and locked eyes with World. She honed in on Maribel's arm movement and knew exactly what her daughter was doing. She seemed to be the only one to notice. She removed herself from the table to use the bathroom.

As World ate, drank, and got his dick jerked off, one of his henchmen came his way, leaned closely toward him, and whispered something into his ear, and World nodded.

"I'll be right back," World told Maribel and the table. He discretely zipped up his slacks, pushed his chair back, and removed himself from the table.

Maribel kept her eyes on him, wondering what was going on. She figured it had to be about business.

World walked behind his goon, and they exited the restaurant briskly. Parked outside was a Cadillac. K'wan climbed out from behind the wheel smoking a cigarette, looking intense. He nodded to World, implying he had something special waiting inside the trunk for him to see.

"Not in front of the restaurant," World told his men.

He got into the truck and followed the Cadillac to a more discreet location in the city, roughly three miles from the restaurant. They pulled into a dark alleyway in the meat-packing village of the city near the West Side Highway. Under the cover of night, cobbled infrastructure, and shadowy streets, World removed himself from the Denali and walked toward the Cadillac.

K'wan got out and popped the trunk. World peered inside and smiled. It was one of Squirrel's soldiers. K'wan had tracked him down and kidnapped him and had worked him over pretty good. He was badly beaten and tortured. He had broken limbs, a bloody face, a broken nose, and cigarette burns all over his body. He was naked with his wrists and feet bound, and a dirty rag was stuffed in his mouth.

"This is one of the muthafuckas that robbed me and killed my niggas, right?" World asked.

K'wan nodded.

World was about to finish what K'wan had started. He lunged down at the man and wrapped his hand around his throat, squeezing his windpipe and making his eyes bulge from his face. He then punched him repeatedly in the face, bloodying his fist and creating more damage to the man's face. World assaulted him until his face started to look like hamburger meat.

"You rob from me, muthafucka?" World exclaimed. "You know who the fuck I am?" He pounded and pounded his fist into his face. "Where is he?" World snatched the rag out of the man's mouth to allow him to speak.

"Fuck you!"

World hit him again.

"Fuck you!"

It was obvious they weren't going to get anywhere with him. World extended his arm out to K'wan, indicating that he wanted the pistol with the silencer at the end of it. He wanted to do the honors. K'wan handed him the 9 mm. World gripped it and grinned.

"Kill me, muthafucka. I don't give a fuck! You a dead fuckin' man too!" the man yelled out.

"All these threats, and all the time, the ones giving them out are the niggas dying. It's them fuckin' first. Shit is becoming redundant, K'wan, Anyway, you first, muthafucka!" World lifted the gun and fired multiple times into the man's head, shooting out his eyes, and placing the barrel of the gun into his mouth and squeezing, blowing out his throat.

It was definitely overkill, but World wanted to send a nasty message to Squirrel.

"Dump that nigga somewhere in public. Make it known who done this shit to him," World told K'wan.

K'wan nodded.

Both men climbed back into their vehicles and drove away. World headed back to his dinner party at the restaurant.

World tried cleaning himself up, wiping the blood from his fists. He noticed specks of blood on his clothing. "Damn! Got this nigga's blood all over me."

"You wanna stop somewhere first, get cleaned up?" the driver asked.

"Nah, I'm good."

The Denali stopped in front of the restaurant, and World got out. Twenty-five minutes had passed since he'd left. He hurried back inside, his clothing looking somewhat disheveled. He had cleaned off the blood from his hand and did the best with the blood on his suit.

Before he joined Maribel's family, he went into the bathroom to splash some water on his face and continue cleaning himself up. He gazed at his reflection.

World smiled at his image. "You go, nigga. Look at you, all handsome and proud. Yes, you are, my nigga. Yes, you are." He chuckled.

He walked out the bathroom with his cell phone ringing. It was Xavier.

"What you want?" World answered brusquely.

"We need to meet."

"When?"

"Tomorrow night, usual spot, same time."

"I'll be there."

"And come alone, World."

"And you do the same."

World hung up. He didn't give Xavier a second thought. He chose not to dwell on the likes of Xavier and his corrupt committee of officers at the moment.

World finally rejoined the ghetto bunch. The table looked like a supermarket had exploded on it, with food and bottles of champagne scattered from end to end. Everyone was feasting on the five-course meal, talking loudly and laughing like hyenas.

World sat next to his woman, like he hadn't just killed a man, and smiled. "Sorry for the delay, everyone. Just had to take care of some business," he said. He turned to Maribel. "You miss me, baby?"

"Is everything okay?" she asked.

"Everything is fine, baby. Let's continue where we left off." He placed her hand on his lap under the table and unzipped his pants.

Maribel began stroking World's dick again while he downed a bottle of Moët. She jerked his dick until he came in her hand, squirting like a fountain. Maribel loved the way he felt in her grip and how his man juices felt across her fingers.

World wiped himself clean with a napkin. "Y'all having a good time?" he asked the family.

"Yeah!" they all cheered, eating and drinking like barbarians.

When the bill finally came, World took care of it. It was $5,800. He pulled out a wad of hundreds from his pocket and dropped an even six grand on the table, plus another $1200, for the mandatory gratuity.

Stepping out into the street, World smiled like a kid at the carnival. He'd had a great meal, a great hand job, a good kill, and a horny woman. Yeah, life was good.

***

Xavier pulled up to their discreet location in the Bronx while World was already parked and waiting. When World saw the headlights approaching, he cocked back his pistol and stuffed it into his waistband. He wasn't about to take any chances. If Xavier even flinched the wrong way at him, he was going to blow his brains out.

He got out the truck and gazed at the black Beamer, its tires crunching the gravel underneath. The vehicle came to a stop not too far from him. The area was still and dark with grass and trees.

Meeting with Xavier was always tense, and meeting him alone was insane, but insane was World's middle name. He'd played house with his bitch for too long now. It was back to business. Now that Luca had apologized to him, he no longer wanted her dead, so that meant Squirrel had to be disposed of immediately.

The two men met face to face under the dark, cautious of each other.

"You are a fuckin' maniac," Xavier spat. "They found a body shot up on the East Side last night. He was connected to Squirrel. Did you have anything to do with that?"

"Do you really wanna know the answer to that?"

"You can be bad for business, World. Do you fuckin' know that?"

"I'm the best business you ever fuckin' dealt wit' . . . the nigga that do the Commission's dirty business."

"Lately, you've been fuckin' sloppy."

"Well, you 'bout to get ya fuckin' wish. When I find Squirrel, I won't play around wit' that nigga this time. I'm gonna blow his fuckin' head off. But before I do that, I'm gonna rob his ass one last time. Pick his flesh down to the bone and skin his ass alive and display that nigga for Harlem to see. Everything that muthafucka brought back to Harlem wit' him, I'll take. Product is low, and I need the cash."

"You need the cash?" Xavier asked with a confused stare. "You're a fuckin' shame, World."

"Why the fuck you call me out here, Xavier? To mock me? Huh, nigga?"

Xavier didn't want to tell World his true intentions. He needed Squirrel alive to take care of Luca once and for all. She had to be silenced. A lot of people she was extorting were worried that their dark secrets were going to be revealed, and the fact that these high-profile figures had been outsmarted by a young girl was embarrassing to them. The contract had been green-lit, but they didn't want her dead until the incriminating footage and photos were destroyed. Xavier was the man they needed to get the job done.

"I need Squirrel alive this time. So you need to fall back off him," Xavier said.

World was confused. "What the fuck you talkin' 'bout, Xavier? A few months ago you were begging me to kill this muthafucka. Now you talking 'bout you want the nigga alive?"

"Yes, you stupid muthafucka!"

"Watch your mouth," World warned.

Xavier smirked.

"I need the payday."

"Why? You goin' broke already? You're spending it all on that young bitch you fuckin'! Sixteen years old. That's statutory rape, you kiddy fucker."

World scowled. If Xavier talked about Maribel again he would tear his throat out.

"I handed you a fuckin' empire, World—gave you locations, product, power, and you got it crumbling already? How stupid can you be?"

"Watch how you fuckin' talk to me," World growled through his clenched teeth, stepping closer to Xavier.

Xavier didn't back down. His eyes met World's. "You are nothing but a hired fuckin' gun. You are not a businessman. You are a loose cannon."

"And I can easily go *bang!*"

Xavier chuckled. He wasn't easily scared. "Don't take it personal, World. Some of us are meant to be kings, and some are only meant to be pawns. But I take it you're not very familiar with chess."

"I never cared for the game."

"And that's why you will always be a pawn. Men like Squirrel take their time building empires from the bottom. They started out as corner boys and worked their way to the top. He established his connect with the Colombians, had a product that was untouchable, perpetual clientele, and loyal soldiers. You, you don't know how to build shit. All you do is take, which I found useful for a moment.

But, like a dog, you bite the hand that feeds you, and you will get put the fuck down."

World didn't give a fuck what Xavier had to say to him. No one was the boss of him, and no one controlled him. He didn't need to build anything. Starting from the bottom to the top took too long. He didn't have that kind of patience.

"Why do you want Squirrel alive now?"

"That is none of your concern," Xavier answered nonchalantly. "Your only concern is not fuckin' with me or the Commission. You've been given a reprieve for now, but I don't know how long it will last, with your recklessness."

World grimaced at the remark made against him.

"Back off from Squirrel. We need him to finish something for us," Xavier warned with his intense stare.

Chapter 19

Clyde huffed and puffed, feeling his nut brewing as his lady propelled herself up and down on his hard dick. He was trying to get back his sex life. He wanted to feel like a man again, and having sex was one way of doing it.

"Oh, baby. Oh shit! You feel so good," he cooed.

Phaedra rode him as he lay flat on his back, cowgirl position—it was the only position Clyde could perform well in. It was their second time having sex. Clyde took his time. His body still felt frail, and he was still rehabilitating.

He panted in her ear, "Ooh, you feel so good, baby." He felt her clamping around him and was ready to explode.

Sex took his mind off his troubles, his pains, and Luca. He had been thinking about her a lot recently, but he didn't let his thoughts known to Phaedra, who'd been there for him every single day. She spent her days helping him with everything and her nights running his lounge.

Phaedra felt his dick pounding inside of her. She needed the sex too. She needed the blissful escape from her chaotic life.

Feeling Clyde please himself inside of her was her brief escape from thinking about the gun charges lingering over her head. She was worried about jail time. Her lawyer was steadily postponing her trial date, but there was only so much he could do. Prosecutors were willing to give her a plea bargain. If she pled guilty to the charges, the best they could do, with her priors, was a two-year sentence with probation afterward. It was a lot to think about. Her lawyer was advising her to take the deal, because he felt there was no way they would win a trial. Phaedra continued to keep everything a secret from Clyde.

"Fuck me!" she cried out.

Her body grinded with Clyde's, their sex and sweat saturating the bedroom sheets. He took his time, wanting to fuck her harder, but he didn't want to push his body past its limits. He had to pace himself. He was still a recovering gunshot victim that could barely walk. But with an intense rehabilitation program, he felt his body becoming better.

He came inside of Phaedra, grunting and panting, letting every ounce of his sperm discharge into her.

She smiled. It was nice. She loved pleasing him. And he took care of her.

Phaedra gently rolled herself off him and stared up at the ceiling. Clyde looked spent and seemed to be in thought about something.

"You okay?" Phaedra asked.

"I'm fine."

He didn't feel like talking, and she knew not to press him. Whatever he was thinking about, he refused to share it with her. It bothered her somewhat, but she chose not to make a big deal out of it. She got up to use the bathroom.

After his nut, she felt strange. For the past week she had been throwing up and feeling nauseous. Her stomach had been doing cartwheels, and a faint feeling would sometimes come over her.

Phaedra looked at herself in the mirror. She took a deep breath and splashed some water on her face. She felt changes happening to her body. It suddenly dawned on her that she might be pregnant. So much had been going on with her life, she couldn't remember when she had seen her last monthly.

***

The next day she went out and bought a pregnancy test, and her suspicion was confirmed. The pregnancy test said she was pregnant. Phaedra sat on the toilet for a moment taking in her situation. She was going to have a baby and might be going to jail at the same time. With her lawyer no longer able to postpone jail any longer, it looked like she might be giving birth behind bars. How was Clyde going to react? Would he stick around? So many questions plagued Phaedra.

Several days later she went to the doctor, and he informed her that she was ten weeks pregnant. It was clear that Clyde was her baby's father. It was also clearer that her child and Clyde would be ripped away from her life for two years if she took the plea deal the prosecutor was offering her. How was she going to be away from them for that long?

"I need to be a part of my child's life while it's young," she said to herself.

Clyde needed to know the truth before it came out on its own, even though she was fearful that he might become enraged and leave her. She had done so much for him, but her secret could no longer go on.

***

Clyde was now walking with a cane, moving slow, but moving around step by step. He stood by the bedroom window gazing outside with a despondent look. He and Phaedra were fucking more often, but he still couldn't stop thinking about Luca. He missed her and thought about her regularly. It had been forever since he'd heard from or seen Luca. Things became so twisted between them, it felt like nothing was going to ever unravel. She had threatened him, but Clyde understood she was upset. What woman wouldn't be?

As he lingered by the window, Phaedra appeared in his peripheral view. She came into the room, holding something in her hand. She seemed downhearted about something. Clyde leisurely turned to face her. "Something's wrong?" he asked.

She looked his way, connecting her troubled stare with his concerned gaze. She was extremely nervous while looking at him. Clyde walked her way with his cane and his limp. Phaedra took a seat at the foot of the bed and lowered her head.

When her tears started to fall, Clyde took her chin into his hand and gently lifted it to meet her stare. "What's going on with you, Phaedra? Talk to me."

She opened her fist and revealed the home pregnancy test.

He peered at it for a moment. "You're pregnant?"

She nodded. "Doctor tells me I'm now three months."

"I'm going to be a father?"

"Yes."

Clyde's aloofness was concerning to Phaedra. He didn't jump for joy or comfort her with language like, "It's going to be okay," or "I'm going to be there for you. We are going to be a family."

"This is astonishing."

Astonishing? Phaedra thought to herself. *What the fuck is astonishing about having his baby?*

Phaedra did have options like abortion or maybe adoption. Twelve weeks pregnant and she was going to be incarcerated in no less than two months.

Clyde fixed his eyes on her. "What you plan on doing?"

She wanted to keep it. She planned on keeping it. She couldn't help thinking, if Luca was pregnant with his baby, would he be asking the same questions? Would he be acting so cold to the news?

She looked at him and decided there was no way around telling him the grim news. "I need to tell you something else," she said in a low monotone.

"What is it?"

The truth just swiftly poured out of her mouth. "I tried to kill Luca."

Clyde thought he'd misheard her, but she repeated it.

"What are you talking about?" he asked with a befuddled stare.

She confessed everything to him, telling the unadulterated truth about plotting to murder Luca. She went on to tell him why she wanted Luca dead, that she was extremely jealous of them, and that the day he woke up out of his coma and called her name, an uncontrollable rage gripped her.

"I'm in love wit' you, Clyde."

Clyde clenched the handle around the cane tightly, almost snapping it to pieces. He heard her speak, but couldn't understand it. She had almost killed the woman he was in love with.

Phaedra was far from done with her confessions. She went on to inform him about the possible jail time she might have to do. She talked about the gun charges and the plea bargain with the prosecutors.

Clyde pivoted away from her direction with his cane and walked toward the window. He couldn't stand to look at her for the moment.

"I just needed to let you know, baby," Phaedra cried out. She got up and followed him to the window.

Clyde's face tightened. He turned her way and said, "Don't worry about it. I'm still here for you, just like you've been there for me."

His words brought comfort to Phaedra. She managed to smile. "Are you serious?"

"Listen, you said that they're trying to give you two years. It's not that much time, and I'll take care of the baby."

Phaedra was ready to jump into his arms and love him. She couldn't believe her ears. After everything she had given up for him, sacrificed to make him well, he had to return the favor. He was a man with morals, even though lust sometimes got the best of him. He had to be there for her and his unborn child.

Phaedra was ready to turn herself in and do the two years. First thing tomorrow morning, she was going to contact her lawyer and take the plea. Her heart weighed heavily on her decision, but with Clyde promising to be there for her and their baby, it eased a lot of the tension she was feeling.

That night they made strong, passionate love again. Phaedra wanted to savor every moment of his kisses, his hugs, feel his body pressed against hers, and the long strokes inside of her womanhood.

Her life was starting to become meaningful, even with her doing the two years. She was confident that after doing her time, she would have a family waiting for her with open arms.

Chapter 20

Wrapped up in a coat and smoking a cigarette, Luca peered at her Brownsville neighborhood from the rooftop of her grandmother's building. It was the first day of spring, but it still felt like winter. She was thinking about her truce with World, who she started to call on a regular. It felt like things were going back to normal between them, like when they were kids. But she understood she had to be careful. World was still crazy, and anything could still go wrong.

She had asked him if she could come work for his organization. It was a huge demotion for her, going from a general to a worker in her cousin's empire, if she could call it an empire. She had to remain humble, though. It was her move on the chessboard, and she was only playing with a few pieces. But the thing about the queen, the most powerful piece in the game of chess, is that it could move any number of squares vertically, horizontally, or diagonally. Nobody was fuckin' with her. Even the king was limited and sought protection from the queen.

Luca stayed on the rooftop. The moment of solitude gave her clarity. Her mind was always her weapon. From the day she had started in the game, her intelligence and wit saved her.

She took a few pulls from her cancer stick, admiring how the hood looked from above. It seemed peaceful from the skies. The projects didn't seem like a nightmare or a spreading plague of violence, murders, drugs, and disease.

Luca thought about the home she once had in Rockaway Park. She didn't forget about the men who burned it down to the ground and took everything from her. They were still on her hit list. She didn't forget about Squirrel trying to kill her in front of her boyfriend. He would soon get his too.

As she waited, she thought about her father. It'd been over a month since she last visited him. She hadn't written him. And he hadn't written her. She didn't stress it, though. The main thing was that she had finally gotten to meet the man.

The door to the roof swung open, and Luca spun around. She was carrying her pistol and was ready for anything. When she saw World stepping onto the roof, she relaxed. He'd come alone.

It was one of their planned meetings.

Their eyes met. He noticed the pistol in Luca's hand and smiled. "Damn, cuz, you definitely have changed."

"Yes, I have," she replied coolly.

Luca put the pistol away. She was ready to unfold her genius into his organization. If she played her cards right, she would be back on top, ruling the throne with an iron fist, becoming the queen bee of it all. She wanted her own cartel. And why not? Women stood behind powerful men for decades, but times were changing, and bitches were no longer serving as props to powerful men. They were taking charge, showing a woman could be just as smart and ruthless as any man.

Luca proved that. She just needed her cousin to trust her again. And when she stared into his eyes, she saw a man ready to burn anything down to clear his way to achieving absolute power on the streets. However he couldn't achieve that without her help.

"I want it all, cuz," World said, a crazed look in his eyes. "I wanna show these muthafuckas that I'm not just some stupid, mindless thug. I want the fuckin' world."

"And you can have it all, World, if you do things the right way."

"And what is the right way?"

Luca was ready to strategize with him. "The right way is patience."

"You sayin' I ain't got fuckin' patience?"

"You ever heard the story of two bulls standing on the hill gazing down at a herd of cows? One is young, the other old. The young bull says, 'Let's run down there and fuck us a cow!' The old bull turns to him and says, 'No, let's walk down there and fuck them all.'"

World was confused by the parable.

"What I'm saying to you, World, is you always been impatient, out of control. Yes, you have a violent name, but you don't have power like I've seen with other men. You're that bull ready to run down and fuck one cow, trying to get that instant gratification, when all you need to do is walk down casually and fuck every last cow in the herd. They don't even see you coming."

"All this talkin' 'bout fuckin' is making me horny," World joked.

"That's the problem with you men—y'all let pussy control y'all. Y'all see a big butt, a pretty face, and a nice smile, and y'all fuck up. You know how many niggas I trapped because of pussy? I extorted over a dozen high-profile officials in this fuckin' city, World—judges, prosecutors, lawyers, police lieutenants and captains, and more. They all fell victim to my scam because they were stupid and thought with their dicks and allowed themselves to be pulled into a web they couldn't get out of. And I was that spider coming down on them, ready to drain them fuckin' dry."

"I could respect that."

World pulled out a Newport and lit it up. He moved closer to the edge and peered over. Heights didn't scare him. He peered at the lights of Brooklyn stretching for miles and marveled at the structure. Harlem was just business for him, but Brooklyn was his home. His heart. He loved everything about it. And it felt good to him that a Brooklyn nigga was dominating Harlem like a champ.

Luca went on to advise him about his operation. As he smoked, he listened. He not only needed to sell weight, but he needed to sell for a higher price. He was practically giving it away. Luca stated that he also needed more corner boys, and they needed to be subtle with their drug transactions, to avoid undercover cops and police investigations.

"You also need to expand your horizon. Black people aren't the only ones that like to get high. When I had my operation, I had lawyers, doctors, housewives, CEOs, cops, and businessmen buying from me. And I didn't scare them off. Most white people only want to do business with people that look like them or who won't scare them to death."

"What you sayin'? I'm scary?"

"You need a lot of work."

World didn't take any offense by it.

"But you expand your clientele, and your product goes further, and you make a lot more money. It's always best to start thinking outside of the box. Also, you need to break your organization up into territories, and you should be able to oversee each territory. World, you think everything through, and it all should run smoothly for you. I still have judges and cops in my back pocket. They still owe me, or I can expose them. Extortion, bribery, and blackmailing the right people can become your get-out-of-jail-free card."

World was glad he hadn't killed her. She was smart enough to survive this far. He was already promoting her, saying, "Brooklyn's yours, cuz."

"What you mean?"

"I mean, you run things out here under my umbrella," he explained.

Luca remained nonchalant. It was a great opportunity and a head start for her.

"I supply you with what you need, points off the package. You become a lieutenant in my shit. I need someone smart like you on my team."

With Squirrel back in town, World didn't want Luca anywhere in Harlem. He felt she wouldn't last long with her ex gunning for her. He also didn't tell her that he'd ignited the flame in Squirrel's heart against her. She didn't need to know all of that. He was going to kill Squirrel soon anyway.

Luca accepted the position, and their relationship was sealed. They talked briefly after that, and then World went on his way, leaving her on the rooftop pondering her next move.

***

K'wan was waiting outside the project building posted up against his Cadillac, smoking a cigarette. It was always good to be back in Brooklyn, and it was better to be the muthafucka in charge. Even though World was paying him and his brother well, he still craved to wear the crown again.

He watched World exit the lobby after his meeting with Luca, and he frowned like he had sucked on a raw onion. He wanted that bitch dead. She had come into his hood and taken over with her Bad Girl product, pushing him out. Now to his understanding, World was allowing her to keep breathing, arguing that she was family and of more use to him alive than dead. K'wan was against keeping her alive. He thought they'd had an agreement. But it was clear to him that World was steadily contradicting himself.

"How everything turn out, boss?" he asked.

"Everything's picture-perfect," World replied.

"So she's still breathing, huh? Why?" K'wan asked in an irate tone.

World was about to climb into the SUV but stopped when he heard K'wan. He glared at him. "Yes, she's still breathing, and I gave her Brooklyn to control. You got a fuckin' problem wit' that, K'wan?"

"Nah, ain't no problem, boss. You running things."

"I thought so. Now take me back to Harlem. I gotta meet wit' my bitch for this blowjob."

K'wan nodded and got behind the wheel, resenting World's choice.

Chapter 21

After a cold and brutal winter of record-breaking snowfalls and frostbite temperatures, warmth was finally in the air, at least for the week, according to the forecast. The leaves could be seen blossoming on the trees, the leaf buds getting fat on the twigs, and flowers looking like they wanted to grow and display their colors. It was early April, and things were changing. It was a different season. A different feeling.

Luca was still staying at her grandmother's place under the falsehood that she was free from the drug-dealing lifestyle, that she had stopped her sinful ways, and would go back to school and better herself. Lucinda believed her, or she wanted to believe in her granddaughter. Luca had looked into her grandmother's eyes and lied her way to keep from being evicted. She only had to hide her transgressions better from her grandmother.

She started moving bricks for World. He took her advice to heart and started to restructure his organization. First, they needed a steady connect. World couldn't depend on robbing and murdering drug dealers for their stash. It became too risky, and they stirred up the police and the feds when bodies started to pile up. He also couldn't depend on Xavier. Without quality product and a steady supply, there was no organization or empire to build.

Luca figured it out, reaching out to the Colombians in Washington Heights. Squirrel's old connect. She went through the red tape to arrange a meeting with them. They didn't know her, and they didn't trust anyone. But if she was able to arrange a meeting with Squirrel when she had first started in the game, not knowing a damn thing back then, then meeting with the Colombians should be a piece of cake. Luca knew they respected money, so she was going to show them the money.

She let the streets talk for her. Her name rang bells, so they had to listen. And when some very important people vouched for her to the Colombians, they invited her to meet with them.

***

Luca parked her Subaru Outback in front of the store owned by the Colombians, on Broadway, a men's clothing store with expensive pieces displayed around full-body mannequins in the window out front.

With the weather finally breaking, and it being a warm day, the area was bustling with traffic and shoppers.

Luca and Meeka climbed out of the car and walked toward the store, which was also used to launder drug money. Luca wore skintight True Religion skinny jeans and a t-shirt meant to be casual, but on a body like hers, everything seemed provocative and enticing. She carried a leather briefcase and a business attitude. Meeka followed behind her dressed in blue jeans and a plain jacket.

They both were armed and nervous. Hearing about the Colombians' ruthless way of making people disappear made them tread lightly into the store, which wasn't busy at all.

A female employee greeted them the minute they walked inside. She smiled and uttered the rehearsed phrase, "Hello, and welcome to Suit and Tie. Can I help y'all ladies?"

Luca looked at the woman. She was young, definitely Latino, and beautiful with her light-caramel brown skin, light-colored eyes, and silky light-brown hair. She was dressed nicely in stylish jeans and a halter top, her curves and hips showing through the jeans, and her breasts protruding through the shirt.

Luca walked over to the woman and said, "We're here to see Horne."

At first, the girl showed no familiarity with that name. "You have the wrong place, ma'am. There's no one here by that name."

"We were asked to come," Luca said sternly. "And we plan on not leaving until we meet with him."

She looked at Luca and then Meeka fixedly. "Just give me a minute," she said.

Luca wasn't in any rush. They lingered in the store, looking around.

The female employee got on the store phone to make a phone call. She talked to an authority figure on the other line, announcing the arrival of two females asking to see Horne. She nodded. "Uh-huh. I understand. Okay."

The brief phone call ended, and she turned her attention back to Luca and Meeka. "He will meet with you."

Luca smiled.

"Walk toward the back, make a left, and down the stairway to your right," she said, pointing to the back of the store.

Luca and Meeka walked toward the back. Luca gripped the briefcase tightly. In it was a quarter of a million of World's money. He trusted her to make the deal. She was becoming the brains, and he was definitely the brawn. She was becoming his number two in the organization, and a lot of people were unhappy about that.

Luca and Meeka made it to the back of the store and followed the employee's directions. The back was a storage area cluttered with boxes and clothing scattered everywhere. To their right was a steel door.

Luca tried to open it, but it was locked.

Perched above the door was a security camera watching their every move. Luca looked up at the camera.

The door buzzed open, and the ladies made their way down into the basement. When they got to the end of the stairway, what they saw was crazy. It was a whole new world—a brothel undern the clothing store. Whores and well-dressed clientele were everywhere. The women were mostly Latina, and the men white, black, Jewish, and Asian.

The décor was one large playroom with a home theater complete with projector and large screen showing hardcore porn. There were two big mirrors on the side of each wall. The golden living room set sat beautifully on the tan carpet near two simple white lounge chairs, creating an intimate sitting area, and there was a labyrinth of rooms used for sex and other pleasures.

Luca and Meeka were met by a beefy guard dressed in black. He searched them and removed their weapons. He already knew who they were there to see. He pointed in the direction where Horne was waiting for them.

Down the hallway to their right was an office.

Smiling, they moved through the area coolly as men locked their eyes on them. Luca wasn't about to tolerate any disrespect from anyone. They kept it moving until they reached the office door, where an armed six-foot-five, 300-pound bearded goon stood guard.

He knocked on the door, indicating to Horne that he had company. The girls walked into the well-furnished office with its nice couches, flat-screen TV, mahogany desk, cigarette smoke souring the air. They met three serious-looking men seated composedly around the room.

Luca walked into the room with her game face on. She observed as all eyes were on them. Moments like this, she missed Phaedra having her back. Not that Meeka was a punk; it was just that she was used to Phaedra.

The main man to talk to was seated behind the mahogany desk, reclined in a high-back leather chair and puffing on a cigar. He eyed Luca intently. He was six feet tall with a lean body, narrow, clean-shaven face, and forceful eyes. He was wearing a wife-beater and cut a Godfatheresque figure, cigar shoved in the side of his mouth and tattoos etched on both arms.

"*A tiempo y hermosa,*" he said in Spanish. "Have a seat." He gestured to the chair placed opposite of him behind the desk.

Luca sat. They looked at each other. There was a titanium gold .357 Desert Eagle on the desk. The gun was huge. Luca glanced at it.

Horne noticed her eyes on the gun. "You like it?"

"I've never seen a gold gun before," she replied.

He smiled, quickly picked up the gun, and pointed the gaping barrel directly at her, his finger on the trigger.

Luca didn't cringe. She looked down the barrel and kept her cool. Easily, he could take her life and get rid of her body somewhere far.

Meeka glared at Horne. She felt helpless.

Horne placed the gun back on the table and said, "I never fired it before. It's simply for show, but it does work."

"Impressive," Luca replied nonchalantly.

"Yes, it is. Cost me fifty thousand. It would be an honor to be killed by this gun. It's handcrafted, and the bullets are gold too," he said smugly. "But, anyway, we are here to do business, not a gun show. You have heart, Luca—Or are you just a stupid bitch trying to play around in a grown man's game?"

"I play well with others, Horne, and I would love to start playing well with you," Luca replied in a sweet tone.

Horne laughed. "Oh really?" he responded. "I don't meet with just anyone."

"And I'm glad you took the time out of your busy schedule to meet with me. I appreciate it."

"Your name has been ringing out lately."

"I like to ring bells." Luca smiled glibly.

"And you've been ringing a lot of bells, even some wrong bells. So why should I do business with you?"

Luca placed the briefcase on his desk, unlatched it, opened it, and swiveled it in his direction to show him the quarter of a million dollars inside. Then she said in a gruff tone, "Because I like to make money, and I know you do too."

Horne gazed at the cash and nodded. "I must say, I'm impressed."

"You should be."

"But you know our business has been with Squirrel for a long time now."

"Fuck him! He's on his way out."

"And you're so sure about that?"

"Sure like I'm betting on a race horse about to win. Squirrel, he's the long shot. He's long in the tooth, and believe me, you keep investing in him, and you'll continue to lose money like you've done before."

"But he's paid his debt with us, fortunately for him."

"And what happens when he fucks up again or gets himself killed?" Luca asked.

"You come in here flashing money, and you expect us to trust you?"

It was time for Luca to pull out her trump card, the one she always used to get her way. It was the same card that snagged Squirrel back into doing business with her after everything went to shit. It was the same card she had shown her cousin. Now, it needed to be used with the Colombians. What the Colombians wanted was a guarantee that when shit hit the fan she wouldn't snitch on them. They had all the money in the world. What they respected most was loyalty.

Luca removed a manila folder from her bag and placed it on the desk for Horne to look at.

"And what's this?" he asked.

"A little incentive for you," she answered.

Horne picked up the folder and took a look inside. They were pictures of men doing drugs, rough sex, kinky sex, violence, and also pages and documents of men cheating on their taxes, their wives, embezzling from their companies, and committing many indiscretions that, if leaked, would ruin their lives.

"These are photos of judges, prosecutors, the District Attorney, cops, and other high-ranking muthafuckas I have control of. They fucked up when they got into bed with my girls. I also have video and lots of copies, just in case something happens. I know who to call," Luca said with a smug smile on her face.

"How did you attain such incriminating evidence on these men?"

"I'm a computer hacker. If I want to know something, I'll go in and take it," she said.

Horne reclined back in his high-back leather chair and took a long, hard look at Luca. He puffed on his cigar and said to his men in the room, *"Es una pieza de trabajo. Yo creo que ella tiene una polla más grande que todos nosotros."*

The men laughed.

Luca said, "I know I'm a piece of work because I choose not to fail. And, as the biggest dick, you fuck me, and I'll fuck you."

Horne was shocked that she understood Spanish. "You speak the language, I see."

"I learned it a long time ago."

Horne sat erect now, seeing how sharp and shrewd she could be. He placed his elbows on the desk and clasped his hands together. He looked her dead in the eyes, and a quick silence descended on the room.

She started, "I—", but then she corrected herself, "my partner and I, we're able to move twenty kilos a week from you. I have a strong network set up, from Connecticut to North Carolina."

"That is a lot of powder to move weekly."

"I've had a lot of practice doing it. I used to buy from Squirrel, but he's become irrelevant. Now I need to buy from you."

"Fifteen a ki," Horne stated.

"Twelve," Luca responded. "And I'll throw in a judge and a federal prosecutor, all yours to blackmail."

Horne chuckled. He didn't reply right away. Their eyes met.

He reclined in his chair and said with finality, "Done!"

Luca smiled. The connect was cemented. She pushed the briefcase closer to him, and they shook hands.

Before her exit, Horne said to her, "Welcome to the major leagues, and I'm giving you fair warning—Bitch or no bitch, you fuck up, we come find you, and when we find do, you'll wish we'd never had this meeting. *Comprende?*"

"I understand."

***

Having sealed a connection deal with the Colombians, Luca felt almost like she was on top of the world again. But she was still under World's umbrella. She was smart enough to know the consequences of dealing with the Colombians directly, but it was worth the risk. She had to earn enough cash to make other major moves. It was a nerve-wracking experience, but she was moving her way up the food chain.

She was keeping a low profile this time by living with her grandmother and not buying anything extravagant or gaudy. She and her crew were rebuilding the Bad Girl brand under World's tutelage. She was helping him make Bad Boy a brand name too in the other boroughs. Business was spreading out like the wind, and she was learning from her mistakes.

World's crew started realizing they were taking orders from Luca. Most were okay with it, but a few hated her and wanted her out of the way. K'wan, who felt he was second in command, subtly led the mutiny charge against her.

Over the months K'wan had firmly worked his way into their structure, killing and dealing drugs for the organization, obtaining World's trust and respect, and now that Luca was on the scene and in World's ear constantly, he wasn't even a distant third. He kept griping with World about his issues, but he wasn't getting anywhere with the boss, who was too distracted by Luca and Maribel to care.

***

Luca had heard from Meeka that Phaedra was in jail on gun charges. She had been incarcerated on Rikers Island and was facing two years. Luca tried not to care, remembering that Phaedra had tried to murder her.

But, lately, she had been thinking about her former friend. When she had heard the news, one part of her wanted to run to Clyde and see if he was all right. Another part of her wanted to take a trip to Rikers Island to ask Phaedra if she really could have taken her life.

Luca noticed the hesitation on Phaedra's face that day. While Phaedra had become a ruthless killer for her, when it came to taking her life, Phaedra couldn't pull the trigger so easily. If Luca wanted revenge, she could have easily gone after Phaedra with all her might. But she hadn't, so she felt that there was still some love between them.

***

Luca walked into the McDonald's around the corner from her grandmother's building on Rockaway Avenue. She ordered her regular breakfast—sausage and egg biscuit with a hash brown—and sat near the window to enjoy the beautiful mid-April day.

She looked like a plain Jane in shapeless sweatpants, white Nikes, and a pullover sweater, her hair pulled back into a long, bushy ponytail. She didn't want the extra attention. She looked like a geek and portrayed herself to be meek.

Nestled in a booth at the back, she got on her laptop to conduct her business. The place was busy with customers coming and going in the morning, but she tuned them out and absorbed herself into the Internet and her work, every so often observing her surroundings.

She was running a criminal empire and moving dozens of kilos for World and once again building her own structure. Money was coming in by the boatloads, so she needed to launder it. With everything that had happened with Dominic, it was hard for her to find an attorney, banker, or CPA she could trust.

She planned on learning everything on her own. She was smart enough to do her own research, coming up with front companies and businesses that only dealt with cash. She had come this far without doing any jail time and planned on going a lot further. World wasn't smart enough to do it. He didn't even have half the information Luca did.

For the past two weeks she had been leaving her grandmother's apartment with her laptop and her concealed pistol and walking into the place for breakfast and some time away. Spending time at the McDonald's became routine for Luca. She also knew it was risky living the lifestyle she was living and venturing alone in Brownsville without any security, but she refused to be afraid and hide out. She moved through the neighborhood like she was penniless and dressed like her clothes came from the Salvation Army.

"I see you always come back for me," she heard Kevin joke.

Luca peered over her laptop to see the manager of the McDonald's smiling down at her with his pearly whites showing brightly, spreading his affable attitude. Her deadpan gaze back at him didn't drive him away. Her rejections didn't either. Kevin was persistent, continually asking her out on a date since the first day he'd laid eyes on her.

He was wearing his signature uniform, black Dickies pants, a gray shirt with his name tag on the right side of his chest, and black nonslip shoes. "You are too beautiful to just sit here alone day after day on your laptop."

Luca ignored him. Even though he was cute with his short, curly hair, smooth black skin, and thin goatee around his full lips, he was still a square, and she felt it could never work between them. He was a low-income worker at McDonald's for Christ's sake. Their lifestyles would clash. It would be Detective Charter all over again.

"I see you favor the VAIO," he said. "Good laptop. I have one myself."

Luca glanced at him again. She had to admit, his attitude was magnetic. Finally, she said to him, "It's been two weeks now, and I'm always ignoring you, but you keep coming at me. Why do you keep trying?"

"Because I always believe in chance, and I like what I see," he replied.

"You like what you see. You don't even know me."

"I remember you."

"You remember me? From where?" Luca asked with an arched eyebrow.

"When we were kids, you used to be alone and always reading. You were skinny back then wearing hand-me-down clothes, and your hair used to be wild. The kids used to tease you a lot, but I used to look at you and admire you. I saw the books you were reading—sci-fi, mystery, history. You were smart, and I admit, I had a crush on you when we were kids."

Luca was somewhat taken aback. She had no recollection of him at all.

"I remember your friend too. What was her name? Nandy? Nisa?"

"Naomi."

"Yeah, Naomi. I never did like her."

Neither did I. She smiled. She looked at his name tag. "So you're Kevin."

"Yup, that's my name, and don't wear and tear it out. But I can get used to you saying my name, *Kevin*; it sounds better coming from a woman's lips."

His jokes were so lame, but his character was friendly and refreshing.

"Don't quit your day job to become a comedian."

"What? You think I'm not funny?"

"You see me laughing?"

"Okay, okay. But I know I can make you laugh."

"There's not much that can make me laugh today."

"Why not? I mean, a beautiful woman like you, you gotta have romance and some humor in your life. But you're cute. Can I keep you?"

Luca chuckled.

"See, the corners of your mouth turned upwards, and I like what I see."

"With me looking like this?" she responded.

"Hey, the simplest things can beget the best beauty."

Luca blushed at his comment. "You think you slick. I see you got some game in you for a burger flipper."

"Call me Parker Brothers. And as for flipping burgers, we all gotta eat, right?"

"I'll tell you what. Since you like to play games, I'll play a game with you. If you can tell me what the acronym on my computer stands for, I'll give you the time and day, and you can have a seat with me."

"Including having one date with you?"

Luca thought about it. She figured it wouldn't hurt. It was only one date, and he looked like he wouldn't get the acronym of VAIO right.

"Okay, I'm ready. Let's roll the dice and see what comes about."

He looked at the VAIO symbol on the computer and looked stunned and confused at first. "I only get one try?"

"One try." Luca smiled, sure he would get it wrong.

"Okay, one try. Here it comes. The acronym VAIO stands for, um, it stands for Video Audio Integrated Operation," he said proudly.

"I'm impressed."

"Glad to impress you. But I have to be honest with you. I'm sort of a computer geek myself. I have three laptops, and I'm going to school for computer science and technology."

"So wait. You mean, being a manager at McDonald's wasn't your lifelong dream?"

Kevin chuckled. "Now I see you're the one with the jokes. I might be rubbing off on you."

"I doubt it."

He slid into the booth seated opposite of her, making himself comfortable around her. "By the way, since I got it right, you owe me a date."

Luca had to respect his diligence. He was a man that saw what he wanted and went after it. She closed her laptop. He didn't need to be in her business.

"You won't get in trouble by talking to me?" she asked.

"Trouble? From who? I practically run this place. I can get you all the free cheeseburgers and Big Macs you want."

"I bet you can. So you're drunk off power. The big man in here."

"Are you making fun of me?"

"No. But you know I'm not a cheap date."

"And I'm not a cheap person," he countered lightly.

Without her realizing it, she was having a cool conversation with Kevin. Like her, he was intelligent, but he was funny and had such a positive outlook on life. That moment at the table, in such a troubling neighborhood and her life revolving around harrowing figures, he made her forget about her own troubles.

"You don't wanna get to know me," she said. "I'm not what you think."

"And I'm not what you think," he replied. "But you're everything I imagine." He saw her statement as a joke, not knowing he was in the company of a deadly queenpin.

Luca gazed into his eyes and she saw that same innocence and rooted simplicity inside of him. He still lived in that bubble, while hers was popped long ago. *It must be nice living without having to look over your shoulder and not having a target on your back.*

Kevin told her about his dreams of owning his own franchise, going to school to get his degree, and living life with dreams and imagination. It was nice. But he was poor. He wasn't what she was used to. However, she accepted his invitation and was ready to go out on a date with him.

***

The first date they went on, Kevin took her to the movies, and the Olive Garden afterwards. Luca was used to five-star restaurants and luxury trips out of town. Kevin made the best of things. It was simple, but she enjoyed his time.

She remembered when she was once a simple person herself, before Nate came into her life and lavished her with gifts. Then came his demise, and she took over from where he left off.

Then there was Squirrel. Her love affair with him was turmoil from day one, but she loved him. And after Squirrel, the accountant Ryan, and a one-night stand with some young buff whose name she couldn't remember, Detective Charter came in the mix. She had liked him, but she wasn't in love with him. Luca found herself trying something different, and it turned out to be a disaster and she almost lost her life. He was a cop, she was a criminal. How could she ever think it could've worked between them? It was a stupid decision on her part. That tragic night still haunted her.

Kevin was different. His easygoing and friendly attitude was rubbing off on her. He talked to her like she was the most important person in his world. He was romantic. He liked holding hands and taking long walks in the park. He loved a good conversation and good humor.

On their second date, Kevin cooked a scrumptious meal for Luca at his place. It was soul food— collard greens and baked macaroni, pork chops, and a delicious tri-colored salad. No man had ever cooked for Luca. They dined at his small project apartment in Brownsville. He was definitely living on a budget, but she overlooked his shortcomings and focused on the good things about him.

Then they went to a Beyoncé concert at Madison Square Garden. Luca had a great time, and after the concert, they walked around and explored Times Square on a beautiful spring night and had dinner at Planet Hollywood.

They also went out dancing at a nightclub. He had two left feet, but he still tried. Luca loved the way he held her on the dance floor when a slow jam came on. He gripped her like he didn't want to ever let her go. Kevin was mild-mannered, always smiling, always positive, and a great person to be around.

Then one night they made strong, passionate love at his place. He tasted the softness of her lips. Their tongues danced together as they lay naked in bed. Kevin was in awe at her nakedness—her curves were like the letter *S*, and her dark pink, luscious nipples looked enticing. He was eager to enter her temple and please her just as much as she would please him.

Kevin couldn't stop kissing Luca. Her kisses were nourishing his passion. It was like she was a sensual fruit and he was savoring every inch of her with his mouth, his lips, and his tongue. He submerged himself underneath the covers and kissed her neck, her shoulders, her stomach, her thighs, her clit, and her hips.

The way Kevin touched Luca was out of this world. He made love to her with his hands at first. He was gentle and passionate, every kiss and every touch mattered to him.

Luca spread her legs, her pussy lips laying out as an invitation. Her juices were flowing freely.

Positioning himself between her legs, Kevin grabbed his dick and placed the head at the entrance to her pussy. He gently thrust himself into her. He moaned, feeling her pussy encase his erection. Lights danced behind his eyes. He wanted to drive himself deeper inside of her.

"Damn! Ooooh shit!" he cried out, feeling the sensation of her wet pussy envelop him. His heart was racing, and waves of pleasure consumed him.

Luca's eyes were rolling back in her head. He had a nice size, seven and a half inches, and a thick width. Her legs wrapped around him, and she grabbed his hips and pulled him to her. "Fuck me!" she said.

He gave her more. Their bodies became entangled and meshed together like a hot iron against a shirt. He fucked her deep and slow and hard. He could feel her pussy grabbing him and throbbing.

Luca was sweating and chanting. "Ooooh fuck! That feels so good. Please don't stop." She was highly aroused and on edge and had a glazed look in her eyes. She continued pulling him on top of her.

He wanted nothing more than to push her legs back to her chest and drive his dick inside her until his cream coated her insides.

They flipped over in a quick change of position, and she slammed her pussy down on his hard dick and rode it to near orgasm, making eye contact with him, using her muscles to milk him.

Kevin reached up to play with her nipples, and her juices coated him. He groaned. His hands were all over her body, cupping her breasts, squeezing and pinching her nipples. He was inside of her with the latex around his dick, and her pussy was so good, he felt like he had nothing on. The feeling of her muscles working his erection made him shut his eyes and bite down on his bottom lip.

"I'm coming," she said.

"Come on this dick!"

Luca loved it. She rode him, moving her hips back and forth, up and down, like a pleasure ride. She could feel him inside her stomach. There was nothing holding him back; this was fucking like it was meant to be.

They found themselves reaching the point of no return. He couldn't hold back any longer, and she couldn't either.

Kevin grabbed her hips and delivered his essence inside of her, shooting his semen into the condom as they exploded together.

Afterwards, he collapsed beside her, his chest heaving up and down as he stared at the ceiling. She nestled against him and placed her head against his chest, and they fell into a deep, comfortable sleep.

***

Kevin woke up before Luca. He smiled at her, watching her sleep. He had no desire to get up and do anything. He just wanted to lie there and be protective of her. She was a wonderful woman, and he was having a wonderful time with her. The past two weeks had been exceptional. She was a busy woman, but somehow she always made time for him.

He gently pressed his lips to her forehead and whispered very softly, "I love you."

Luca stirred a little, but she didn't wake up. She was sleeping like a baby, looking ever so peaceful.

Chapter 22

Squirrel climbed out of bed naked, his dick swinging and still dripping with Angel's juices. He had just fucked her like an animal, and now she was fast asleep. He removed a Newport from the full pack, lit it up, and took a deep drag. He needed the nicotine. He felt it seep into his system.

It was the middle of the night, and the place was quiet. He was staying in the Bronx at an undisclosed location. Harlem was too hot to rest his head, and Brooklyn was a hazardous ground. He put on his boxers and went to the window. He gazed outside and looked at the darkness as if it was some iconic wonder.

As Squirrel peered out the window, he frowned. Word on the streets was that Luca had hooked up with his Colombian connection and struck a deal. He didn't want to believe it. He figured Horne, being a cautious man, wouldn't associate with anyone so readily. But Squirrel also understood that Luca could be very convincing and influential when she needed to be. She had snagged him, and he didn't even know the bitch. He only knew she was Nate's bitch back in the days. But she was a black widow—and one of the deadliest bitches he'd ever encountered. She was exceedingly smart and manipulative. If Squirrel knew back then what he knew now, he would have beheaded her long ago, but his weakness had always been the flesh. The same thing that made him laugh was now making him cry.

It bothered him that Luca and Horne were in business together. It complicated things. He was back in Harlem dealing with his old clientele, and almost everyone was welcoming him with open arms. He was becoming the man again, despite major interference from World. But he was determined to take that monster down. Harlem wasn't big enough for both of them.

Squirrel looked at the time. It was three a.m. He had a few of his men strategically posted around his location for his protection. When he heard about his soldier Spike getting shot multiple times in the head and his eyes shot out, he realized World was going to be a more difficult problem than he'd first thought. Squirrel couldn't go through the front with the nigga, so he devised a plan to go around the back and attack from there. He was going to make it so that World didn't even see the attack coming.

As Squirrel lingered by the window, his cell phone went off. Angel stirred in her sleep, hearing the chime. Squirrel quickly answered it.

"Yo, who this?" he said roughly.

"It's me. I figured you would want to link up and talk about our mutual problem," the caller said.

"I didn't think you'd call back," Squirrel said.

"I'm calling back now."

"When and where?"

"Meet me at dawn, three hours from now. There's a diner in Yonkers. It's safe, no eyes, no ears. And World's people don't stretch that far."

"A'ight," Squirrel replied, writing down the directions.

The caller hung up.

This is it. Squirrel smiled.

World was about to fall, and it was happening from within his own inner circle. Squirrel wasn't the only one who wanted to see that crazy muthafucka dead. Some of his own peoples thought he was pushing too far and making wrong decisions. He had heard that World and Luca reconciled their differences after all their drama and conflict, and that he even put her over some of the niggas who had been loyal to him since day one. It seemed like a coup d'état was about to take place.

Squirrel finished off his cigarette and climbed back into bed with a naked Angel. He nudged her awake and said roughly, "Let me get a fuckin' blowjob. I need one right now."

Angel looked at him with a slight attitude but quickly complied. Squirrel propped his head on the pillow as Angel descended beneath the sheets, pulling out his erection and taking him into her mouth.

"Oh, I need this, baby," he said. "A nigga is stressed."

"I got you, baby. I always will."

Bad Girl Blvd 3

***

Morning was cracking open the sky. The early-hour travelers were on their way to work via public transportation or private vehicle. The black-on-black Escalade came to a stop at the quaint diner on the Boulevard in Yonkers, New York. Squirrel rode shotgun, pulling on his cigarette and looking around. He wasn't used to being up so early, but he looked forward to this meeting. This was the opportunity he had been waiting for.

Carmine's Diner was nestled in the middle of the boulevard. It was a popular place, known for its desserts and soul food.

Squirrel climbed out of the SUV with his pistol tucked into his waistband and flanked by two of his goons, including his cousin Homando. They walked into the twenty-four-hour diner and sat in the nearest booth. The place was empty except for one waitress and the cook all the way in the back.

Squirrel slid into the wooden booth and sat facing the exit. He could never sit with his back toward any doorway or exit. His biggest fear was being shot in the head from behind. However, the relaxed décor of the diner with its plants in the corner and vases on each table eased him some.

The waitress was warm and hospitable to the thugs. "Would y'all like to start off with drinks?" she asked them.

Squirrel ordered coffee, and his men ordered some tea. His men picked up the menus to order, but Squirrel wasn't hungry. He steadily looked around waiting for the meeting to happen. It was a non-smoking environment, so he needed to drink some coffee to keep awake and focused.

Ten minutes later a burgundy Cadillac parallel-parked outside. Squirrel fixed his eyes on the car, knowing it was K'wan's. K'wan and Dwayne climbed out of the car and proceeded toward the diner. He keenly watched their every movement.

"They're here," Squirrel said.

He and his men straightened up and got serious. K'wan and Dwayne were extreme killers also, and anything could pop off at the drop of a hat.

When they got to the entrance of the diner, the brothers paused on their way in. K'wan motioned for their meeting to happen outside.

It wasn't a problem for Squirrel. He and Homando exited the diner and met with the brothers.

"Let's walk, just you and me," K'wan suggested.

"Let's walk then," Squirrel said.

The two coolly walked away from the diner and started their meeting. Both men lit up cigarettes and moved a half a block away from the diner.

Squirrel asked, "Were you responsible for Spike's death?"

"I had a hand in that," K'wan answered honestly.

Squirrel frowned. Spike was a friend, and as much as Squirrel wanted to murder K'wan, he had to put his emotions to the side and remember what was more important—World's downfall.

"It was only business wit' me; nothing personal," K'wan said nonchalantly.

The men stopped walking and faced each other. They had all the privacy they needed, with the streets bare of any vehicular traffic and pedestrians. The sun was still rising and fresh in the cool morning sky.

"You and I both want the same thing," K'wan explained.

"And why's that?"

"I never liked that muthafucka anyway. He and his cousin ruined me in Brooklyn. I'm on his team, moving up in his organization simply because he helped out my little brother. Besides that, he's no use to me. World has got to go, and if you can make that happen, you can have Harlem back. All I want is Brooklyn."

"They say he's the devil," Squirrel said. "And many have tried to kill him, even me, and he's just hard to kill."

"You should know that any muthafucka can get got."

"And he will get got. I just don't want to fuck this up."

K'wan told Squirrel, "I know his routine. I know his main bitch and his ways. Together, we can set him up."

The two continued talking, and K'wan ran down information about World, and Luca too.

Squirrel was itching to take action. First on his list was Luca. He'd failed once trying to kill her, but he wasn't going to fail again.

Chapter 23

World couldn't fight off the bizarre feeling developing inside of him. It struck him rapidly like a speeding bullet. It wasn't the first time he'd felt this way. He was spending quality time with Maribel in their project apartment, sexing and talking, when suddenly he became ill. His stomach felt like it was twisting into one giant knot with a throbbing pain, and he had a high fever. He developed an agonizing headache, became weak and ill overnight. When he started throwing up and could barely breathe, Maribel rushed him to the hospital, where he was seen by a doctor in the emergency room.

At first food poisoning was suspected, but that wasn't the case. The doctors couldn't pinpoint what was exactly wrong with him. He was quickly treated, got better, and released a few hours later with some prescriptions to take for his illness.

However, a week later, World developed the same illness, feeling much worse this time. He felt faint and nauseous. He had no idea what was wrong with him.

He couldn't function once again. He was in a stage of paranoia. He couldn't eat because he was always throwing it up and had diarrhea.

Maribel became extremely worried about him. Once again, in the middle of the night she rushed him to the hospital, and he was seen in the emergency room. This time the doctors kept him overnight and ran some tests, taking his blood and trying to analyze his illness.

Once again, it was hard to pinpoint his illness. World got better within a few hours, and he was released.

But his running in and out of the hospitals and the doctors not being able to come up with an accurate diagnosis was becoming troublesome to him and Maribel. World thought that maybe it was stress.

Maribel thought it was something much more serious and sinister. Some demonic force was trying to take away her man. She couldn't sleep at nights, not knowing what was going on with him.

On his third trip to the hospital, he had difficulty breathing, a fever, a chronic cough, nausea, and tightness in the chest. Heavy sweating followed. This time Maribel had to call 9-1-1, and he was rushed to the nearest hospital via ambulance with paramedics treating him en route.

This time the doctors decided to keep him longer. They admitted him into his own room. He didn't have health insurance, so everything was being paid for in cash. This posed another problem. Healthcare was expensive, but World was effortlessly coming out of his pockets to pay for the best treatment, and that could trigger an investigation.

Maribel stayed by his bedside as hours passed and World wasn't himself.

***

Luca decided to pay her cousin a visit. She walked into Harlem Hospital on Lenox Avenue and went up to the fourth floor to visit him alone. There, she finally came face to face with Maribel. Luca had heard about World's sixteen-year-old girlfriend. She couldn't believe her cousin would stoop so low to fuck this young bitch.

Luca was displeased with their relationship, and expressed herself freely about it, saying things like, "Fuck that young ghetto bitch," and "I don't know why my cousin got with that tacky bitch in the first place," or "She's a fuckin' gold digger."

Luca walked into the room to see Maribel seated by World's bed as he slept. Maribel looked up to see Luca stepping into the hospital room. The two girls locked eyes, and immediately there was tension between them.

Maribel stood up and frowned. Luca gazed at her, looking annoyed that she was only using her cousin.

"Bitch, you got some fuckin' nerves comin' up in my muthafuckin' man's room!" Maribel exclaimed.

"I ain't here for you," Luca replied calmly. "I came to see how he was doing."

Maribel shouted, "Bitch, I know you out there talkin' shit 'bout me! I don't give a fuck if you like me or not. You fuckin' wit' the wrong bitch."

Luca wasn't about to argue with a sixteen-year-old child. She was packing heat and was ready for the confrontation. She had killers for bitches like Maribel.

"I don't give a fuck if he's ya cousin or not. You ain't fuckin' welcome here, bitch!"

"Fuck you, bitch!"

Luca clenched her fists as Maribel hurried her way looking for a fight, but nurses and security charged into the room to break them up before it escalated. It took two security guards to hold back Maribel from lunging at Luca, who showed a lot of restraint. She wasn't worried about Maribel.

The conflict woke up World, who had no idea what was going on. He saw Luca and Maribel shouting at each other as security and staff roughly escorted them out of his hospital room.

Outside, Luca took a deep breath and tried not to let a ghetto sixteen-year-old girl frustrate her. It was her cousin's business, but she understood how pussy worked. It could get a nigga caught up; stop him from thinking rationally. She needed World thinking rationally, at least for now.

The confrontation wasn't over, though.

Maribel came rushing out of the hospital front entrance, her beady eyes intensely fixated on Luca, who was standing on the curb. She gripped a sharp razor and was ready to slice Luca open with it. She ran her way, shouting out, "I'ma fuck you up, bitch!"

Before Maribel could attack, Meeka and Brooklyn sprung out from the parked SUV with their guns drawn and aimed at Maribel, halting her violent charge.

Luca smirked. All she had to do was give the order and Maribel would be blown away. "Yeah, bitch, recognize who the fuck I am," she said with an attitude.

"Fuck you! This ain't over, bitch," Maribel spat.

Luca whispered through her clenched teeth in Maribel's ear, "It is today. Now take your ass back into that building and be by your man. You're way out of your league, Maribel. I don't like you, and I never will, and I know you can't stand me. But, bitch, fuck with me again, and you won't even see your death coming."

Maribel retreated back into the hospital, scowling heavily and making threats at Luca.

Luca climbed into the back of the SUV with her crew and they drove away. With World in the hospital for a few days, Luca felt it was only a matter of time before everything fell into place.

***

They'd only had sex once, but their love was growing. Kevin was an honest man, a hard worker, and he was different. Her relationship with him was gradually growing, but she felt indifferent sometimes with him, because she couldn't stop thinking about her past.

She had recently started thinking about Clyde more often, and the fact that her track record with men wasn't so good made her question herself and her relationship with Kevin. Would he change on her, like so many others who had come before him? He seemed like the perfect type of guy, even though he wasn't financially able to provide for her and protect her from the streets. He was more book-smart than street-smart.

She knew he wouldn't be able to handle the secrets she kept from him. She was haunted by the way Detective Charter had flipped out on her so suddenly when he came across the truth. Clyde had rejected her, and Squirrel had abused her love and trust. With every male came some kind of issue, so Luca couldn't help but wonder what it would be with Kevin.

She ran his background, and he didn't even have a speeding or parking ticket. Everything about him was legit. His parents were retired and living in Florida, he had no brothers or sisters, and he had no kids.

Kevin was patient with her. When the streets called and she had to leave abruptly during times of intimacy, he always seemed to understand, even when she couldn't give him a decent excuse.

When she spent time at his place, he continuously gave her deep oil massages, ran warm bathwater for her, and cooked for her around the clock. Their conversation was at all times profound. Luca always went to his place. He never went to see her.

She had lied about her source of income, telling him she was collecting unemployment from her previous job. In his eyes, Luca was struggling to make ends meet most times, like him. He wanted to take care of her.

Kevin had no idea she was wealthy. He was caught up. This time, Luca decided to play it smart. She was stacking her paper, making hundreds of thousands of dollars in secret while living with her sick, elderly grandmother. Her money was now hidden in safe deposit boxes. No more hidden rooms.

Nestled in his arms watching a good movie on cable, Luca felt his warmth, love, and character so much, she didn't want to be let go.

She started to think about Clyde again. Why was she thinking about him all of a sudden when she had a good man ready to love her? Then she thought to herself, Clyde knew everything about her, from her past to what she was about on the streets, and he accepted her. Kevin only knew one side of her, and that was the meek, lying side. She wondered, if Kevin knew the truth about her, would he become frightened and leave her? She wrestled with the decision whether to tell him or keep it a secret as long as she could.

Kevin got up and went into the kitchen. He came back out, got down on one knee, and said to Luca, "Will you marry me?" He smiled his golden smile, holding the ½ ct diamond engagement ring he must have spent his entire two checks on.

Luca was stunned. She didn't know what to say. She couldn't say yes because it was too soon, but she didn't want to lose him either. She still had issues and baggage from her past she needed to deal with.

"I can't right now, Kevin."

He looked heartbroken. "You don't love me?" he asked reflectively.

Luca sighed heavily. "I do, but it's too soon, and there are some things you need to know about me."

"Like what? I know you're a great girl, and if it's about the money, I know it's hard right now, but we can make it work. I'll get another job. I know I can support us," he said with confidence.

"I need time to think and get some things straight."

Kevin nodded. "I understand, and I'm willing to wait as long as it takes you."

Was it right to lie to him, knowing that her violent, drug-infested world could come back and haunt them both? The people she associated with and dealt with would eat Kevin alive. He was too nice to have anything happen to him.

They talked and came to a mutual understanding. It could wait.

Luca left his place knowing before she moved forward with Kevin, she had to see one man in her life. She had to confront him. She couldn't stay away from him any longer.

She exited out the lobby with the dark above her and walked toward her car. She got behind the wheel and lingered for a moment, her head spinning. After so many tries and so many years, was love truly in the air for her? Did she find the right man this time? He didn't come with much, but his heart and his love was more wealth and riches than any kingpin could give her, and he respected her.

Luca started her car and merged onto the moving traffic on the Avenue and drove in silence. She traveled three blocks from Kevin's place and came to a stop at a red light. She sat at the light with the car idling, her purse with the .380 inside on the passenger seat. She didn't pay too much attention to the black Yukon that had stopped next to her Subaru.

The windows to the Yukon rolled down, and the threat suddenly became bona fide. Two outstretched arms came out the window, one gripping an Uzi and the other a 9 mm.

Luca turned and became wide-eyed. Abruptly, her car was being shot up, and glass shattered around her. She screamed, ducking into the seats. She could feel the bullets tearing her car apart and whizzing by her. There was no time to reach into her purse and grab her pistol, which was no match for the Uzi spraying her car with a hail of bullets.

She pushed her foot against the accelerator and floored it, thrusting the Subaru through the busy Brooklyn intersection blindly and barely missing two oncoming cars. The car hit fifty with her barely having control of it, and then she felt the thunderous crash. The car shook violently, soared in the air, and slammed back down toward the pavement. She had hit something at high speed, but she didn't know what it was.

Luca tumbled around the front seat. She could feel the car was mangled, probably twisted around something. She was afraid to lift her head and inspect her safety. She heard screaming and people coming to her aid. Her purse had slid onto the floor and was covered with remnants of glass. She snatched it up and pulled out her gun.

Slowly, Luca lifted her head to observe her surroundings. She was in shock and shaken up. She was still alive somehow, and the gunmen were long gone. Her car had wrapped around a street pole and toppled it over. The car was totaled.

Luca had to climb out the passenger window that was shot out. She landed on her side on the ground and was immediately aided by Good Samaritans.

"Ma'am, are you okay?" someone asked.

Luca was helped to her feet and looked dazed for a moment. Miraculously she was only grazed in the arm and suffered a few cuts from the glass shattering around her.

A crowd of witnesses started forming.

"You need a hospital," one female said.

"We've called nine-one-one."

"Just relax and everything's gonna be all right."

Everyone was telling her to lie down, be calm, that the police and ambulance were on the way. Luca heard them, but she didn't have time to talk to any police officers or go to any hospital. She refused to be cooperative.

She pushed her way past everyone, exclaiming, "Get the fuck off me! I need to go!"

It took a struggle, but Luca managed to leave the scene of the accident. She hurried toward a gypsy cab stopped at a red light and jumped into the backseat. She could hear police sirens blaring in the distance. The gypsy car drove off with Luca in tears. She was grateful she was still alive.

The small crowd of people gathered were dumbfounded by Luca's suspicious actions.

Luca knew the hit had to come from Squirrel. Her cousin was no longer a threat, and Phaedra was locked up. There were no more playing games. Now it was time to get revenge.

The cabbie drove her to a motel in Canarsie. She didn't want to go to her grandmother's house. There was no telling if the killers were there waiting for her, and she didn't want to put her grandmother's life at risk.

Until Squirrel was taken care of, Luca had to stay away from the people she loved, including Kevin.

Chapter 24

World was on bed rest for a couple of days and still healing from his sickness. For him, it felt great to be home. Maribel was by his side taking care of him. For a girl that was sixteen years old, ghetto and loud, she showed loyalty and concern to him, sticking with him through sickness and health. Whatever he needed, she was there to take care of it. If he needed her to kill for him, she wouldn't have hesitated in doing it. She wasn't just about talk, but about her business. Every day she was proving her love for him.

Sick or not, there was still business to take care of. The news came to him about the attempted hit on Luca in Brooklyn. He was glad Luca survived. World figured that the contract on his cousin's life came from either the Commission or Squirrel. Either way, they both needed to be taken care of and taken out. It wouldn't be too long before they came gunning for him. He had to be ready for the inevitable.

Luca called him to tell him what he already knew.

"Don't worry 'bout it, cuz. I'll personally take care of it. I'll kill Squirrel myself," he assured her.

"Nah, fuck that. I want him myself."

"You sure you can handle it?"

"I've been handling my business for a long time, World. I even dealt with your shit. So don't fuckin' insult me by asking if I can fuckin' handle it. I got my killers on standby."

World chuckled. She had definitely transformed into someone else. He remembered the day an emotional and ambivalent Luca came to him for help with killing Nate. The naïve look in her eyes couldn't prepare her for the consequences after putting a hit out on the boyfriend. World thought his cousin would never last, thinking she wasn't built for this game, but she proved him wrong time after time. World was impressed by her tough demeanor. Not too many people could survive a hit like that. She was a survivor and she was a fighter.

Maribel frowned after Luca hung up.

World was aware that his bitch and Luca were at odds with each other. He'd heard about the incident at the hospital that trickled out into the street.

"That bitch had her peoples point their guns at me, and you defending that bitch?" she argued. "She talks shit 'bout me on the streets, slandering my fuckin' name, and you think she right? I wished they killed that bitch!"

World cut his eyes at Maribel. "She's still family!"

"Fuck that bitch!" Maribel shouted out. "It wasn't too long ago when you hated that bitch and y'all were warring wit' each other. She disrespects ya bitch—me—and you claiming she family? Are you fuckin' stupid, World? You trust that fuckin' bitch?"

"Who the fuck you talkin' to like that?" World countered.

He was bed-resting, but he was still in charge. He propped himself up against the headboard and glared at Maribel. She didn't answer him. World was still a man she didn't want to push over the edge, because if so, he would take a handful of muthafuckas with him as he was falling.

She loved him and she was sure he loved her, but he was a crazy muthafucka that most times didn't think before he reacted. Maribel knew she had probably said too much.

"C'mere," World asked, motioning with his index and middle finger for her to come closer to his bed.

Maribel approached slowly and cautiously. Their eyes met.

World said, "Don't you ever talk to me like that again. Bitch, I'm the one running this fuckin' show, and she's family."

"I'm ya family," she uttered in an importunate tone.

"You are family, but she's business. Don't you forget that."

Maribel didn't respond. She was jealous of Luca and didn't trust her at all. She knew that bitch was up to something. World didn't see it, but Maribel had that woman's intuition that something was wrong. But World had the last words for now, and she would continue to love him. He took care of her and her family graciously, and that was something she would never forget or take for granted.

***

Luca still had some love for Squirrel, even after he'd made two attempts on her life and failed. It was like she had nine lives. However, their sexual history and her drawn-out love for a man who had taken her for granted and wanted her dead wasn't enough to spare his life. She sent the dogs out to hunt, Meeka, Brooklyn, Chin, and Scotch. They were thirsty for blood. They took care of Luca, and she took care of them. She put the word out that she wanted Squirrel dead.

She hacked into police computer files to search if there were any warrants out for Squirrel. She also hacked into top-quality surveillance footage of the tri-state area. Squirrel was somewhere, and there had to be some footage of him. Day and night, she was on her laptop, pulling up information.

She decided to dig up all of the surveillance footage of the attack on her in Brooklyn the other day, obtained from nearby businesses and homes in the area. *Bingo!* She found the Yukon on camera.

She zeroed in on the license plate and ran it through her system in the DMV.

After meticulously looking into everything, she found out Squirrel had a cousin named Homando, who used to be in the military. She became a detective, or more like a bounty hunter. Luca wasn't going to rest until she found Squirrel and had him killed.

She also figured that Squirrel wasn't stupid enough to stay in Harlem or Brooklyn. So where could he be? Where would he feel safe at? The Bronx? Queens? Long Island? New Jersey? Or Upstate?

The license plate came back to a residential address in Jamaica, Queens. She sent Brooklyn and Chin to investigate, and they drove out to Queens the next day.

Luca didn't forget about the landlords that burned her house to the ground and made her lose everything. Months had passed, and now it was time to extract revenge.

The Kabakoff brothers lived together in a waterfront condo in New Rochelle. They'd committed insurance fraud and gotten away with it. Or so they thought. She had suffered because of their greed. Once she pinpointed their location, she sent Scotch and Meeka to handle it.

***

The Kabakoff brothers emerged from their lovely beachfront home on an attractive spring day, both men handsomely dressed in tuxedos and wingtip shoes, and wearing their yarmulkes. They walked toward the parked Lexus, all smiles and laughter on their way to a traditional Shabbat dinner at the synagogue a few miles away.

They climbed into their car and started the ignition. Suddenly, there was a tap at the driver's side window and a young, baby-face goon appeared.

The older brother rolled the window down and asked, "Can I help you?"

"Yes, I'm lost and I need direction," he said.

"Where are you headed?"

The young goon pulled out some directions written on a napkin and asked, "Where can I find Pelham Road?"

"It's not far from here. What you can do is—"

The Kabakoff brothers were ambushed by intense gunfire and instantly killed with multiple shots to their heads, and their bullet-riddled bodies lay slumped over the steering wheel and the dashboard of the car.

Scotch and Meeka hurried toward the idling car and sped away.

Two down, now one to go.

***

Squirrel sat in the barbershop chair on Merrick Boulevard in Jamaica, Queens. The hip-hop-themed shop with its flat-screens and the pool table in the back wasn't crowded. Four barbers methodically worked on their clients' hair. Squirrel got a shape-up and chatted with the barber Tony, a ruthless ex-drug dealer from Harlem who had the streets on lock back in the eighties and early nineties until his incarceration. He did a ten-year stretch for drugs and guns, got out several years ago, and turned his life around.

Tony brought Squirrel into the game, took him under his wing, and mentored him when he was in his early teens. Squirrel had learned from the best.

Queens had always been an unfamiliar place to Squirrel. It was out in the boondocks, so it didn't have that gritty feel like Harlem did. He hated Queens. It was too quiet and too residential for him. He only came to visit Tony and get a haircut.

Tony was broad, black, and muscular, with a bald head, high cheekbones, and a sharp chin. He wore boot-cut jeans, beige Timberland, a T-shirt, and a gold chain adorned his neck. He had no piercing or tattoos. Tony always believed distinguishing tattoos and long hair made you a target for the police and an investigation. He'd reigned over Harlem for years because he kept things simple. It was something he steadily tried teaching Squirrel.

"What's this I hear about you having problems in Harlem?" Tony asked. "They said you went down to North Carolina. I thought you left for good."

"Ain't any problems, Tony. I got everything under control."

"I keep hearing about this World muthafucka. I still keep my ears to the streets, even from way out here in Queens. And they talk about this man like he's some kind of bogeyman."

"He ain't no bogeyman. He just a dead nigga wit' a fuckin' gun, Tony. Any nigga can be got."

"Yeah, if that was the case, why he pushed you out your own neighborhood and had you run like a bitch to North Carolina? And a Brooklyn nigga too."

Squirrel felt like he was being chastised by his former mentor. He frowned and clenched his fists. Everyone was talking, and he was looking more like a bitch the longer World was breathing.

Tony swiveled his chair around so he could look Squirrel directly in his eyes. "Look, I retired from the game a long time ago for a reason, and I'm not trying to be in your shit. My advice—Get the fuck out now and leave the game to these fuckin' snitches and bitches, 'cuz the game done changed, Squirrel. Niggas ain't built like you and me anymore. You have beautiful kids and a beautiful woman. I hope you had some sense to save up your cash and move on."

"And then what? Have my name tarnished out there and have this nigga make me look like I'm a scared fuckin' bitch? You know me, Tony. I ain't the one to back down from a fight. This nigga come into my town"—Squirrel slammed his hand against his chest to make the point— "and wanna make a bitch outta me? Fuck that! He gonna get got! *And* his bitch fuckin' cousin."

"It's that ego you always had, Squirrel. And that ego is always going to be your downfall."

Squirrel sighed deeply and scowled. "No disrespect to you, but just cut my shit, Tony. I got this. I'm running this shit now, not you."

Tony didn't take any offense. He shook his head coolly. "It's your world now, player. I just hope you survive it long enough to see what I'm talking about."

***

Parked across the street from the Queens barbershop were Luca and her crew, heavily armed with automatic weapons and ready to take action. She recognized the truck out front. It was the same Yukon that had shot up her car in Brooklyn. They didn't even have the savvy to change the license plates.

Luca, Scotch, and Meeka waited patiently. They surveyed the area. Merrick was a busy boulevard, but with evening descending upon the city, traffic was lightening up. Luca felt proud to have tracked down Squirrel.

"We wait until he comes out," Luca said.

They noticed one man in the truck, seated behind the wheel, and a certain snitch named Milky Mike had informed them that Squirrel only had one bodyguard in the barbershop with him. Squirrel was slipping. This was their chance.

Scotch exited the car and slyly placed himself near the back of the Yukon, keeping out of sight from the mirrors of the truck, with a .50-cal. gripped in one hand and his ski mask in the other.

They waited. Luca had a Glock 17, and Meeka carried an AK-47.

Ten minutes later, Squirrel and his bodyguard were seen exiting the barbershop. The area around them wasn't crowded, giving Luca and her crew the perfect opportunity.

Squirrel and his henchman walked toward the Yukon, not knowing danger was lurking. Squirrel answered his phone and started a conversation. His beefy six-foot-three bodyguard walked behind him like he was a giant shield.

The minute they were about to climb into the truck, Luca and her killers masked up and sprang into action. From the back, Scotch took out the bodyguard with several large rounds from the Desert Eagle .50-cal. slamming into his large body and knocking the heavy man off his feet.

Meeka's AK-47 pushed the driver's brains all over the front seat. Squirrel found himself trapped and taken aback by the setup. He dropped his cell phone and tried to reach for his pistol, but he was overcome with two straight shots into his legs from Luca's Glock.

He collapsed to the ground, clutching his injuries and screaming out, "You fuckin' bitch!"

Luca rushed toward him and aimed her pistol at his face.

"I know it's you. Don't do it. Don't fuckin' do it," Squirrel pleaded.

While those hearing the chaotic gunfire hid or ran for safety, Tony came rushing out of the barbershop with a .45 in his hand.

Meeka spun around and trained the AK-47 on him. She had him dead to rights. They locked eyes. She yelled, "This ain't ya fuckin' business. Go back into ya shop."

Tony was in shock. He looked past her and fixated his eyes on Squirrel hugging the concrete in pain and bleeding profusely. He scowled and tightly gripped the .45 in the palm of his hand.

"I know it's you, Luca," Squirrel shouted out.

Luca pulled her mask away from her face, showing him her identity.

Squirrel glared up at her. "I'm sorry, I'm fuckin' sorry."

"Fuck your sorrys!" she screamed. "It was you last week, wasn't it?"

Squirrel was confused by her question. "What the fuck are you talkin' about?"

"You shot up my car at the intersection."

"I didn't do it."

"You're lying!" she screamed.

"I swear to you, it wasn't me! I still got love for you, baby. I do. And, besides, it was your fuckin' cousin that persuaded me to go after you in Brooklyn. When I shot ya boyfriend, my mistake."

Luca scowled. She didn't care about that.

"Luca, hurry up and do this nigga! We gotta fuckin' go!" Meeka screamed out.

"I swear to you, I didn't come at you last week. I ain't had shit to do wit' that."

Strangely, Luca believed him. She hesitated in pulling the trigger.

Squirrel was begging for his life, and oddly, his cell phone was still on and his baby mama Angel could hear the entire ordeal from the other end.

Luca looked at Squirrel one last time and smiled, saying, "I would have loved you forever, Squirrel."

After those words, she fired three rounds into his chest and killed him. She didn't believe he had anything to do with the second attempt on her life, but he had to go anyway. She had to clean out her past and move on to a progressive future.

Tony could only watch. Meeka made him drop the gun. If he hadn't, his blood would've spilled on the sidewalk too.

The girls retreated and sped away.

Luca sighed heavily. There was this part of her that felt relieved but sad too. Squirrel was finally out of her life for good. Oddly, she thought about Phaedra, knowing she would have been happy to see it done. She never liked Squirrel in the first place.

∗∗∗

It was a beautiful day to play golf on Pine Hill Golf Course on Long Island. The Cadillac of golf courses, Pine Hill was a private 18-hole regulation course and country club facility. Its back nine offered rolling hills, elevation changes, dense hardwood forest, and water features, including the creek and a natural waterfall on the signature hole of the day. The unique layout featured undulating zoysia and native grass terrain, two lakes, and bent-grass greens against a picturesque backdrop of exclusive homes and the ocean.

Xavier and his golf-loving associates were playing most of the afternoon away. Xavier was an excellent golfer, and whenever he had the chance, he went out with his expensive golf clubs and teed off with his friends. He was considered a scratch golfer.

He was about to tee off again, clad in black khakis, a collared shirt, golf shoes, gloves, and a visor, looking more like a professional golfer than a member of the murderous Commission.

"Are y'all ready for another hole in one?" he asked.

"Yeah, yeah. Just hit the damn ball, Xavier," another golfer returned.

Xavier chuckled and positioned into his swing, clutching his driver, trying to emulate Tiger Woods' stance, but before he could tee off, he saw a golf cart with two women quickly approaching them. Xavier suspended teeing off and stared at the unwanted company coming their way.

"What the hell is this now? I thought this was a private club," one of his associated griped.

"I don't know," Xavier replied, his attention on the two women.

The golf cart came to a sudden stop, and Luca and Meeka jumped out dressed like they were about to play the game themselves. Luca fixed her eyes on Xavier. It was the first time seeing him. Xavier already knew who she was.

"You must be Xavier, I presume," Luca said.

Xavier equably said, "You're interrupting a private game."

"Oh, I am, huh?" Luca replied, holding a 9 iron in her hand. She walked closer to Xavier while Meeka stood in the background.

Xavier's cohorts stood around in awe. They frowned, wanting the ladies to leave ASAP.

"You know, I could never understand this game, never really got the meaning of it. You swing these expensive golf clubs to try and hit one measly white ball down a lumpy field into one hole. What fun is that?" she said, walking toward the ball and taking over the tee.

Luca used the 9 iron to impressively drive the golf ball down the field. The white ball went soaring into the air and landed a long distance away from them. She smirked. "Oh, I'm sorry. I should not have done that. Did I interrupt an important game here?"

Xavier asked, "What is it that you want?"

"What I want is your fuckin' head," she growled. "I know you put a contract on my life. I know about the Commission, a bunch of corrupt cops running drugs and committing murders. And I'm sure you heard about Squirrel's demise."

Xavier frowned. He didn't appreciate his business being exposed in front of his business cohorts. *How dare she!*

"I'm here to let you know ... don't fuck with me, Xavier. I see you, muthafucka, and now you see me."

Xavier's frown changed into a cocksure smile. "You have no idea who you're fuckin' with."

"I know who I'm fuckin' with. Remember me, Xavier, because I'm gonna be that bitch to take you down. I'm smart enough. I found you, right?"

He chuckled. "You think that, huh?"

"Leave me the fuck alone! This is your only warning. After that, you'll see what I'm capable of," she said through gritted teeth. "And enjoy your game."

Xavier didn't like being threatened, especially by some young hood bitch. He looked at her intensely as she started walking back to the golf cart. He couldn't control the impulse to yell out in front of his cohorts, "You're a dead fuckin' bitch, Luca! You hear me? You're fuckin' dead!"

Luca smirked and went on her way.

Xavier stood there scowling and clutching his driver tightly. He took the golf club and started swinging at his own golf cart, smashing it up. He then flung the club into the air.

One of the men on the course asked, "Xavier, you okay?"

***

Luca had gone to tell World about Squirrel's demise, and she told him she didn't believe Squirrel had anything to do with the second attempt on her life. She was sure of it. The only thing that stumped her was the Yukon with the North Carolina plates.

"It's the Commission then," World had told her.

"The Commission? But the car definitely belonged to Squirrel's cousin. You think he would cross Squirrel and take it upon himself to take me out?"

World nodded.

"But why?"

"Money. The Commission's reach is far and wide. If they want you dead then they will do whatever necessary to make that happen. Ya feel me?"

World had informed his cousin about the Commission. It was the first time she had heard about them. She was confused. Luca used her computer savvy and skills and found out everything she needed to know about them— what they were linked to, who they were, and what they were about. They were killers with badges. She linked Kendall and Poor Billy's deaths that were executed so long ago to the Commission. They were murdered while trying to deliver thirty kilos to New Haven and Hartford, Connecticut.

Luca had lost a lot of money. World had warned her that it was only a matter of time before they came gunning for him and her. Luca wasn't about to go out like that. She was too young to die, and she still had something to prove. So the Commission became a target on her kill list. It was either them or her.

Chapter 25

Kevin wanted to marry her. He was in love with her, and she loved him. Being around him brought her into a place of normalcy. With him, she could forget about her troubles and laugh. She felt like a woman. She felt so loved by him, if anything ever happened to him because of her, she would've been distraught. They'd had sex once. But Kevin, being such a gentleman, was willing to wait until they were married or whenever she was ready again. His heart was so big, you could throw up in the air and it could black out the city.

But Luca had to be sure this was it. Clyde was always on her mind. Some nights she would lay with Kevin and think about Clyde. She needed answers from him. How could he have tossed her aside so easily? It truly bothered her. She needed to see him again. She needed some closure. Even though he'd chosen Phaedra over her, she always felt that something just wasn't right.

***

Luca walked into the Paradise Lounge the next evening looking her best. Her long, gleaming legs were erect in a pair of exclusive Red Bottoms, and her long hair flowed down to her shoulders. It was a lovely spring night, and Luca wanted the attention.

She instantly spotted Clyde working behind the bar. He was standing again, and though he had to walk with a cane, he was healing.

Clyde turned and noticed Luca walking in. He was in awe. The two locked eyes, and he was transfixed, almost dazed.

Luca approached him. His eyes looked sad and happy at the same time. She took a seat at the bar. There was a moment of silence at first. It seemed unreal that she was there.

Clyde broke the uncomfortable silence between them. "You look good."

She smiled. "Thank you."

"You look really good."

"And I see you're walking again and healing very well."

"Yes, I've been enduring a grueling physical therapy program. It's costly, but it's working."

"That's good."

"What brings you here, Luca? I thought you hated me."

"I came to see you. We need to talk."

He nodded. "I'm ready to talk."

"Not here, someplace private."

"We can always go back to my place."

She smiled. "Of course."

Luca knew Phaedra was locked up for gun charges, but she didn't gloat about it. He was now alone, so she figured he was suffering enough.

"You want a drink?" he asked.

"I'll take some wine."

Luca waited patiently for an hour until Clyde was ready to leave. Once his staff had everything covered, the two left together with her car because he was used to being chauffeured everywhere.

***

Back at his apartment, the two sat in the living room and talked.

"Why did you choose her, Clyde?" Luca asked.

Clyde took a deep breath. He intended to be honest with her. He looked at her softly and said to her, "It was a mistake. I only chose Phaedra because I felt you wouldn't be there for me."

"What?" Luca was confused.

"Look at your life, Luca. You're a queenpin."

"And?"

"I thought you could never truly forgive me for sleeping with Phaedra."

"And?"

"And I'm not getting any younger. I've been there and done that. And the attempt on your life, the one I suffered for—"

"And I owe you for that. I've apologized to you over and over, and I was ready to be there for you. I loved you."

"I loved you too."

"So what went wrong?"

"I don't know. I think about you every single day, Luca. I missed you so damn much."

She wanted someone that would be gentle with her heart, to treat it with tender, loving care. It was fragile because it'd been broken too many times. But then she was plagued with certain questions. *Would Kevin accept her into his life if he knew the truth about her? Could he handle the truth?* Clyde could.

Clyde gazed into Luca's eyes like he was seeing her for the first time.

Luca missed his strong, masculine hold around her and the way he fucked and made love to her. She could always talk to him about anything, including the streets, and he was always ready to give her advice.

Clyde inched his lips near hers. Luca needed to feel his lips exploring every crevice of her curvy frame with exacting detail.

They pressed their lips against each other and started to kiss fervently.

Clyde absorbed her into his arms and showered her with kisses, on the nape of her neck, her weary shoulders, down her back, between her legs. He held Luca in his strong arms and smelled her scent. His hands fondled her breasts, massaged the small of her back, then landed on her open thigh.

She pulled her dress up to her hips, revealing she wasn't wearing any panties.

Clyde was ready to penetrate her, ready to feel her goodies once again. His tongue and mouth washed over her body, caressing her, touching all her sensitive places.

Luca's nipples got so hard, they were sensitive to his touch. He played with them, sucking and licking on them like they were small pieces of candy. He drove her to distraction, freeing Kevin from her mind, while he fingered her pussy, stimulating and arousing her with sensual words in her ear.

They decided to continue their action in the bedroom.

Clyde cupped his hands with the fullness of Luca's ass when she wrapped her legs around him, giving him her juicy, wet treasure. She wanted him to make love to her with his very being, to feel his love with every vigorous thrust between her soft thighs, to make her sweat and scream his name. Their tongues danced, as if they were made to be together.

"I want you," he said in her ear.

Luca reached down and cupped his thick, hard erection. She jerked and massaged his dick gently. She loved the way his hard flesh felt in her manicured grip.

Gradually, they stripped their clothes away and became entangled against the silk sheets, their naked flesh wrapped around each other.

Clyde played with her nipples until she was burning with passion. He took his time caressing the softness of her inner thighs with his mouth, moving near her glorious center. He spread her legs as she invited him to explore her erotic fold of femininity and tease her aroused clit gently and softly. She whimpered and pleaded for satisfaction and release. He could feel the slippery wetness, letting him know that she craved for him to be inside of her.

It was a breathtaking sensation when he penetrated her and they became one. Clyde impaled her with his hard flesh, slow and intentionally, deep and hard. She wanted to feel every hot, hard, throbbing inch of him inside of her without any protection.

Luca gasped. "Ugh! Ugh! Ooh! Ooh shit!" She wrapped her legs around Clyde and pulled him closer.

She was dripping with desire for him and so wet, with their bodies colliding in ecstasy, the big dick kept sliding in and out of her. She couldn't think of a better sensation than feeling that thick, hard dick thrusting into her, pumping her, and filling her up.

Clyde whispered in her ear, "Shit! Ugh! Shit! Your pussy feels so fuckin' good. I love you. I missed you."

Her nails dug into his ass, pulling him deeper and deeper inside of her. She craved for him to bury his flesh deeper, harder, faster, to fuck her with all his might.

Clyde rode that pussy like an ocean wave. He sucked on her nipples once again and grinded between her soft, inviting thighs.

They kissed passionately, and then from behind, he grabbed her hips to feel her tits swinging while he thrust with all his might into her pulsating pussy, putting his finger in her ass, the freak that he was.

On top of him, Luca wanted to use his dick like a dildo, making herself come by rubbing her clit up and down the shaft of his dick while she fed him her tits.

Finally, with her legs pressed back and his tongue in her mouth, she longed for that explosive finale. She felt his dick pounding her, leaving no room for error, making her scream with tears shaping in her eyes and ready to receive his precious gift.

"I'm coming," he announced.

"Don't stop! Don't stop! Fuck me! Oh shit! Fuck me!"

Luca came all over his raw dick, splashing his penis with her pleasures, and then Clyde grunted loudly and discharged his fluid deep in her.

They gripped each other, panting and feeling spent.

Clyde held Luca in his arms like he never wanted to let her go. He said to her, "I made a mistake. But I'm ready to correct it." He didn't even want to know if Luca was dealing with someone else or not.

But it wasn't that simple.

They talked and then made strong, passionate love again—in the missionary position. He came in her again.

They nestled closely until midnight came and, for the third time, fucked again. Clyde couldn't get enough of her.

"I love you," he said.

"I love you too," she said.

They fell asleep naked in each other's arms.

Luca had found closure. She understood the reason now. It wouldn't be fair to Kevin when Clyde had made his choice months ago.

***

The following morning, Clyde woke up alone. Luca was long gone. He was stunned. He found a note beside him.

Now I can move forward. Thank you.

Chapter 26

Xavier climbed out of his 3 Series BMW in the underground parking garage dressed in a three-piece suit and carrying a briefcase. He walked briskly toward the elevator with a lot on his mind. His focus was mainly on Luca. The stunt she pulled on the golf course embarrassed him, and his associates wanted to turn their backs on him. He'd underestimated her, but no young bitch was going to outsmart him and embarrass him.

It was that time of the month, the customary meeting with the Commission in their secure and secret location. At the table, his main priority was Luca and World. He gave World a pass because he would need him in the future, but with Squirrel dead and Luca threatening his life, there were no more passes.

Xavier stepped into the elevator and pushed for the top floor. He checked his texts while the elevator quickly ascended. He stepped off the elevator and walked into the room where the council of corrupt officers was already seated and waiting to discuss the month's business. Xavier took his seat at the table and placed his briefcase beside him. He placed his cell on the table.

Captain Clark immediately expressed his concern. "What are we going to do about this bitch?"

"I heard she paid you a visit on your favorite golf course, Xavier," Detective Holden added.

"Gentlemen, everything's under control," Xavier assured.

"She's not stupid, Xavier," Sergeant Ripple exclaimed. "She killed Squirrel, and she is becoming a problem. A fuckin' threat to us!"

"And if she tracked you down so easily, what's stopping her from tracking us all down?"

Everyone was worried and upset.

"We should have killed her and her lunatic cousin a long time ago," Captain Clark said.

Xavier frowned. The men at the table wanted to pay a hit man, whatever his fee, to take out the problem.

As Xavier was about to address the Commission, his cell phone rang. He looked at the screen—anonymous caller. He ignored the call, but the phone rang a second time.

"Who this?" he barked into his phone.

"I warned you, Xavier, to leave me the fuck alone," her voice serenely spoke on the other end.

Xavier cringed hearing Luca's voice. "How did you get this fuckin' number?"

"I have my ways. And I see you don't listen," she expressed coolly.

"Fuck you! You don't know who you're fuckin' with, you fuckin' cunt!"

The Commission was stunned that she had called his phone during their secret meeting. They all looked suspiciously at Xavier while sitting on one butt cheek.

"She found us. Shit, she fuckin' knows where we're located," Lieutenant Greenwood shouted out in a panic. He jumped from his seat and was ready to leave the room.

"Relax," someone told him. "She isn't that smart. We've been doing this for years. You think some young cunt bitch can track us down. We went against the fuckin' Mafia, coldhearted killers, and the FBI. This bitch ain't a fuckin' threat to us."

Luca chuckled. "I hear some unrest going on in your Commission," she taunted.

"You listen closely, you fuckin' bitch—"

"No, you listen. But wait, you don't, and I think you never will. So good-bye, Xavier. It's been fun. Oh, and answer the fuckin' phone in your briefcase."

Luca ended the call, leaving Xavier bewildered.

The minute she hung up, he heard another cell phone ringing. It was coming from his briefcase like Luca predicted. He was dumbfounded.

He slowly picked up the case, placed it on the table, and opened it. Inside was a cell phone chiming. It wasn't his phone. He didn't put it there. A text message was coming through.

"What the fuck!" Xavier opened the text and it read: *Here comes the bang!*

It took him only a second to figure out what the text meant. His eyes widened in fear and panic, and he screamed out, "Everybody, get the fuck—"

KA-BOOM!

The loud explosion violently shook the room, filling it with fire and black smoke, sending pieces of the Commission everywhere. The remote control device exploded from his briefcase. Billowing smoke filled the room. Everyone was dead, blown to pieces. There was no more Commission.

Unbeknownst to Xavier, when Luca left him on the golf course, she had planted a tracking device on his car. She hacked into all of his accounts and figured out his routine. It didn't take long for her to have his briefcase switched with an exact replica. Inside the briefcase, the cell phone was used as a typical remote control to send a signal via radio airwaves. The signal energized a relay connected to a blasting cap, which in turn detonated the explosive material sewn into the briefcase. It was genius.

Following Xavier was the key, and the Commission was handed to her on a silver platter.

Luca sat in the passenger seat of the Lincoln Navigator, peering up at the top of the building, black smoke billowing from one of the rooms. She smiled. Killing her rivals was becoming too easy.

Meeka turned to her and said, "If they didn't know then, they fuckin' know now not to fuck wit' you."

Luca nodded.

***

Angel grieved over Squirrel's death for weeks. She blamed only one person, Luca, and she wanted her revenge. Unbeknownst to anyone else, she was pregnant with his third child. She connected with Squirrel's cousin Homando and decided to take over his organization with Homando's help. She had been around the drug game for far too long to not know what she was doing and how things worked. She knew all of Squirrel's connections and sources, and with Homando's help, she was on a mission to avenge her baby father's death, and Luca was the target.

***

Luca heard about Angel and her struggle to rise in the streets. She laughed and even mocked Angel. It'd been weeks since Squirrel's death, and the bitch needed to get over it. Squirrel got what was coming to him. It was the game; some people played it better than others. He had made his move, and Luca made hers. Fortunately, her move was checkmate.

Luca wasn't worried about Angel or any of her nemeses. When she took out the Commission, it solidified her position in the game and showed just how ruthless, calculating, and evil she could be. People started to fear her a lot more. Not even World saw that one coming.

The streets were talking. Luca was becoming the new power.

However, Luca caught a surprise of her own. She sat in the doctor's office waiting for the results to come back. Lately, she hadn't been feeling too well. She was suffering from headaches and nausea. Some days she would become lightheaded and would have a loss of appetite. Now wasn't the time for her to get sick. She was re-building her empire and couldn't look weak. She feared that some burning sickness was overcoming her. So she immediately went to get checked out, meaning blood work done, her urine examined, her blood pressure taken, the whole works.

Luca sat silently in the doctor's office alone. She took a deep breath, and gazed at all the medical degrees that covered the entire wall, from his master's degree to his PhD. He had numerous family photos throughout the room and plastered on the wall behind his chair, from his kids to what appeared to be his loving wife on his desk. He was a family man. Luca thought about having a family once, but things became too hectic and crazy in her life.

Looking at the certificates on the doctor's wall, Luca wondered if she hadn't become a drug queenpin, if she'd grown up having a better life with loving parents, finished her schooling, had healthier encouragement, then where would she be? She was smart enough to become anything she wanted to be, even a doctor. But fate had something different planned for her. Was this her destiny? She always wanted kids and a family, but that never happened. She was the loyal girlfriend, but she was always cheated on and forgotten.

The doctor walked into his office, closed the door, and took a seat behind his desk. He was an attractive black male clad in a white lab coat with the stethoscope around his neck. He was six foot tall, well built, had smooth black skin with a dark goatee.

He placed Luca's medical chart on his desk and leaned forward with his elbows on the table, his hands clasped together. He looked at Luca.

She became nervous. Did he have some bad news to tell her? Did she contract some kind of STD—*Ohmygod! Was it AIDS?* Did karma come back to bite a chunk out of her ass? She had done a lot of bad things.

Luca's mind started to spin with worry after worry. It felt like her heart was sinking into the bottom of her stomach just waiting to hear her results. It had to be bad news.

"Ms. Linn, you're six weeks pregnant," he announced.

"What?" Luca was stunned. It was the last thing she expected him to say. "I'm what?"

"You're six weeks pregnant. Congratulations to you and the lucky man."

Luca took a deep breath. *Congratulations? This is crazy.*

The doctor continued talking, but she blocked him out.

She already knew it wasn't Kevin's baby; they'd only had sex one time, and he'd used protection. It definitely was Clyde's seed growing inside of her. Six weeks pregnant . . . the time frame definitely added up. It was the night she'd gone to his place and they fucked like rabbits. He didn't use a condom, and he came in her multiple times.

Luca walked out of the doctor's office feeling ambivalent. She always wanted to have kids, but life always prevented that from happening. Now, she was pregnant, and the man she wasn't with, who she had walked away from and didn't want any dealings with, was the father to her unborn.

How was she going to explain this to Kevin?

Luca exited the medical building and climbed into the passenger seat of the Lincoln Navigator with Meeka sitting behind the wheel.

Meeka looked at her and asked, "Is everything cool?"

"Yeah, everything's fine."

She didn't want to tell anyone about her pregnancy yet. She planned on keeping it a secret until the right time. The life she lived wasn't that of a housewife or a married woman who couldn't wait to share the news with loving friends and family. She was a gangstress. A bitch like her couldn't go around sharing news of her condition. It might send the wolves ready to carve her unborn out of her stomach.

"Just take me home," she told Meeka.

Meeka nodded and drove away.

Luca laid her head against the window and closed her eyes.

***

Rikers Island was the last place Luca wanted to be. It was dirty, loud, overcrowded, and intimidating. The jail sat on an outsized island a stone's throw away from the runway to LaGuardia Airport. There was only one way on and one way off the island, a long, sole route bridge to the island for vehicular traffic. It was a fixed, low-level span built with concrete and steel.

The correction officers were scowling and didn't seem to care about anyone's well-being. She was going through the searches where there was signs posted everywhere and the guards making it clear that no cell phones, cameras, or any type of electronic equipment were allowed inside. Everyone was thoroughly searched as they stepped on the premises, and anyone found with contraband would be subject to immediate arrest and full prosecution.

Luca had nothing to worry about. She came simply dressed in a pair of jeans, a T-shirt for the warm summer day, and her white Nikes. No one suspected who she really was and what she was about. She showed her ID and continued on with her visit.

Before she got to the main visiting room, she went through two more thorough security searches where she had to take off her shoes, her belt, and be scanned by a long wand after stepping through the metal detector.

The Rose M. Singer Center was the only female inmate facility on Rikers Island. It featured a nursery with capacity for up to 25 infants. Luca took a seat at the table and waited for Phaedra to enter the room.

Luca sat patiently. The room was filled with female inmates who had mostly family visit them.

Moments later, Phaedra was escorted into the room by a female guard. Luca hadn't seen her in months, since the frost and cold in New York. Now it was early summer, and so many things had changed.

Luca couldn't believe her eyes, seeing Phaedra clad in her prison attire and wobbling toward her, almost eight months pregnant with her hand against her stomach. She was pregnant with Clyde's baby too.

Phaedra was stunned to see Luca had come to visit her. Was it a social visit or a threat? She stared at Luca as she struggled to sit across from her.

"I didn't think you would ever come visit me. What brings you here?" Phaedra asked indifferently.

Luca looked at her former friend and couldn't do it. She had come there to boast and talk shit to Phaedra. She couldn't believe the bitch was pregnant too. Her mind had changed. Seeing her big belly was a shock.

"Is it Clyde's?" Luca asked.

Phaedra nodded. "It is."

"Boy or girl?"

"Boy."

Luca wished she could tell her congratulations, but she just couldn't.

"Do you love him?" Luca asked.

"I do. I really do, Luca," Phaedra responded emotionally.

Luca sighed. She didn't love Clyde anymore, and she had Kevin now. But there was still that tinge of hatred for the woman who stabbed her in the back and betrayed her. Luca decided to keep the news of her pregnancy to herself. It just didn't feel right telling Phaedra.

Phaedra's eyes started to tear up. "I didn't want for any of this to happen, Luca. I just got caught up, and one thing led to another, and then I'm in here. I'm sorry. You were like a sister to me. You were my best friend."

"Would you have pulled the trigger?" Luca asked.

"I don't think I had it in me to kill you. My emotions just came over me," Phaedra said. "Wit' Kool-aid's death and Little Bit, Clyde gave me that little comfort. I was fucked-up, really fucked-up."

Luca believed her.

"If I knew you liked him in the first place—"

"I was in love wit' you, Luca," Phaedra blurted out. "I've been in love wit' you since the day we met. I never could tell you. But I'm telling you now. I love you and Clyde."

It caught Luca off guard. She didn't swing that way and never planned to. She was somewhat glad Phaedra had kept her feelings to herself, but didn't take any offense to the confession. She decided to bury the hatchet. They'd been through too much to continue on with their beef.

"Phaedra, you will always be a friend to me, despite what went on between us. You taught me things."

"You taught me things too. I owe you. If it wasn't for you, I don't know where I would be. I'm so sorry. I got two years in here, but it ain't gonna be the end of me. When I get out, I'm gonna raise my son and start over. And if it ain't awkward to you, I want you to be my son's godmother."

Luca respectfully declined.

It was an emotional reunion between them. Luca left Rikers Island with a feeling of accomplishment. She had rekindled an old friendship, making her list of enemies shorter. She could have easily had Phaedra killed, but there was some love still left in her heart for her friend.

No one needed to know she was pregnant with Clyde's baby too. She would play it off as Kevin's baby.

Chapter 27

Wwhat? You got AIDS or somethin'?" one of World's goons asked him.

World didn't know what was going on with him. He knew he was dying from something. He was weak and almost skeletal-looking, having lost a tremendous amount of weight. Everyone was thinking he'd contracted HIV or AIDS. The symptoms were there.

Even Maribel went to get herself checked out because not once did she remember them using any protection. Her test results came back negative, though. She was grateful.

So what was going on with World? The doctors were still stunned by his illness. He was tired of going in and out of hospitals and would hold court in his apartment while sometimes bedridden.

He went from a monster to this frail and weak man. Even though he was sick, he was still the feared boss running things. He had men so loyal to him, they would still die for him.

Luca continued to bring him packs of cigarettes and tried comforting her cousin the best she knew how. She and Maribel were still beefing with each other and bumping heads. Heated arguments often ensued between them, and even a fight took place. Luca wasn't much of a fighter, so Maribel got the better of her for a quick moment. Luca wasn't going to forget that the ghetto bitch put her hands on her. She was only breathing because of World.

World decided to have a meeting with all of his lieutenants, including Luca. Everyone came to the Bronx apartment. He was resting on the couch with a chronic cough that sometimes made him hunch over in pain and spit out blood. He was looking sicklier every day, but he had a strong will to live.

Eight men, all of World's trusted lieutenants, stood around him with stern stares waiting to hear what he had to say. Luca was standing among the hardcore gangsters in the room. They gave her respect because she had earned it. Taking out Squirrel and the Commission made others think twice before they fucked with her.

Maribel stood by her man's side and constantly glared at Luca, wishing the bitch wasn't in the same room with them.

World got to the point, saying, "K'wan has placed a bounty on my head."

His men became furious.

"World, I told you not to trust that muthafucka in the first place. I ain't never liked him," one of his lieutenants said.

K'wan had plotted with Squirrel to try and take World down. He had placed a high bounty on World's head. The contract was green-lighted, and K'wan was going against the grain, bringing his brother along for the ride.

"I got eyes on the streets," World said. "That nigga pops up anywhere, and he's a dead man."

"We gonna find that snake muthafucka and make him pay," one of World's thugs said.

The contract was put into action—kill K'wan on sight.

World had other news for his men. He coughed heavily for a minute and then got himself together. His sickness was taking a heavy toll on his body. World clutched his chest and tried to breathe. He was hurting. Everyone waited patiently for him to get himself together.

Maribel was by his side nursing her man. Without him, her family would be lost. He was taking care of everyone. If World died, Maribel didn't know what was going to happen.

What he was about to say next would shock everyone.

"When I die, to let y'all muthafuckas know, Luca will take my place. She deserves it. She's smart and ruthless enough to keep this going."

Everyone was in shock, even Luca. She didn't expect World to announce that.

Maribel couldn't believe what she was hearing. "What?" she exclaimed. Her face twisted into rage and jealousy. She glared at Luca and balled her fists.

Luca could only smirk back.

"What the fuck you talkin''bout, World?"

"What the fuck I just say? You wanna fuck wit' her, go ahead. But my cousin ain't nothin' nice to play wit'. She can kill like the best of y'all, and she's smart."

World's crew was shocked, but they all knew he was right. Luca was the only one capable of leading because she had done it before, and she had done it well. In fact, some already suspected she was pulling the strings behind closed doors.

Maribel was so heated. "You pick that bitch over me? Fuck y'all!" She stormed out of the room.

Luca gloated inside. Seeing that bitch upset was the highlight of her day. She kept her composure, though. In her mind, she did deserve it and was going to be back on top. And with World and Squirrel gone, the Commission dead, her connection with the Colombians secured and going well, she would be running things in the entire tri-state area and maybe expanding. It felt good to be that bitch.

They say that the female is the most dangerous of the species, and that extended to the drug game as well. Luca was about to become part of a cream-of-the-crop list, knowing women at the top of drug cartels are a far cry from hapless Nancy Botwin on *Weeds*. Some of the most feared and respected queenpins Luca looked up to were Sandra Avila Beltran, Griselda Blanco, Kath Pettingill, Blanca Cazares Salazar, Thelma Wright, and Mireya Moreno Carreon. Luca Linn was about to join that list.

✳✳✳

Two weeks later, World's condition took a turn for the worse, and he had to be hospitalized. He was placed into ICU. The doctors knew it was only a matter of time before he expired.

Luca took extra measures to make sure her cousin's last days were comfortable. That included not allowing Maribel any access to him. She gloated knowing Maribel wouldn't see him anymore. Her deadly goons made sure of that, guarding World's room night and day. She was in control—the shot-caller.

Only immediate family was able to come and visit him. Maribel and her family were shut out completely. Luca hated them with a passion. She felt they were trying to suck her cousin dry and only took him into their family because he had money and was taking care of them. It infuriated her that they allowed a grown man to have sex with their sixteen-year-old daughter. Luca made sure they got nothing. Not a fuckin' dime.

One evening, Maribel and her ghetto family, every last one of them, came storming into the hospital determined to see World. Their money, their lavish lifestyle, and the pricey gifts and respect because of World had come to an abrupt end. They were poor and struggling again.

Maribel and her family came charging into the hospital to make a scene, but Luca had serious-looking men there to deal with the situation. Maribel and her family were stopped inside the lobby and embarrassed. The scene sent

Maribel running away in tears and heartbreak. She loved World, and not being able to be by his side during his last days tormented her.

Luca sat in the passenger seat of the Navigator watching the whole scene unfold with her men, Maribel's family, and hospital security. It pleased her to see that bitch upset.

A small scuffle ensued outside of the hospital, but it was quickly handled.

A grin appeared on Luca's face. "That young bitch wanna fuck with me, then she gonna learn the hard way who I am and what I'm about," she said to herself.

Chapter 28

Kevin was in the kitchen cooking. He planned on preparing shrimp alfredo, pasta, and steamed spinach. He was great in the kitchen, and had the potential to become a master chef.

"You gonna love what I cook for you, baby," he hollered from the kitchen.

Luca smiled. "I can taste it already," she replied, the aroma hitting her nostrils. She couldn't wait to eat.

She lounged on the couch watching TV in his small apartment. She touched her stomach. She was two months pregnant and hadn't told him yet. In fact, she hadn't told anyone. It wouldn't be long before she started to show. She thought about an abortion, but she had always wanted kids.

Clyde's baby growing inside of her gave her a strange feeling. She was living two completely different lives.

While Kevin busied himself in the kitchen, Luca heard her phone ringing. She looked at the caller ID and saw it was Clyde calling her once again. He was trying relentlessly to get back with her and have her in his life, but she had moved on.

Luca frowned. While Kevin was still in the kitchen, she picked up her phone and went into the bathroom. There she answered his call after ignoring him for so many times.

Luca answered harshly, "Why the fuck do you keep calling me?"

"I need to see you. I miss you so much," he said, sounding desperate.

"I told you, I'm done with you, Clyde. There is no more us. Phaedra is having your baby, and I can't go backwards."

"It was a mistake."

"Yes, it was. You made your choice when you picked her over me and got her pregnant. So fuckin' deal with it."

"I know, and I'm sorry, but just let me explain."

"There is no explanation. We're done. I'm in love with someone else, and I'm having his baby."

The news broke his heart. He'd definitely made the wrong choice from his hospital bed that day. He thought he was smarter than Einstein, but was completely wrong about Luca. She was the one from the start.

"I'm changing my fuckin' number," she said and then hung up on him.

Luca took a deep breath. She had already forgiven him. If he hadn't messed around with Phaedra, she would have loved him with all of her heart. Now he was dead to her. She felt he needed to put all of his energy on Phaedra and their baby and live happily ever after with his choice.

Luca rubbed her stomach and felt some type of way about the situation, being pregnant by a man she didn't want anything to do with. And there was no way she was going to tell him she was pregnant by him.

Kevin knocked on the bathroom door. "Baby, is everything okay?"

Luca sighed heavily. "Yes, baby. I'm okay."

It was time to tell him she was pregnant by another man because eventually he would find out. However, she felt she had to convince him to keep her secret and treat her child as his own. She slowly opened the door, and there was Kevin standing outside the bathroom smiling at her.

She looked at him reflectively and said, "Baby, we need to talk. I have something serious to tell you."

Chapter 29

K'wan got into the passenger seat of the luxury Benz with a 9 mm tucked into his waistband and another weapon secretly holstered around his ankle. Dawn was approaching, and it was looking like it was going to be another beautiful summer day. He had been keeping a low profile, hiding out at his girlfriend's place.

Dwayne was driving the Benz, and Paquitta was sitting in the backseat. K'wan knew he was a marked man. He was on high alert and wasn't too trusting. He moved in silence and was ready to shoot on sight if he thought anything was out of place. The only people he trusted being around were his little brother Dwayne and his girlfriend Paquitta.

With Squirrel dead, K'wan knew he was next on the list. Dwayne had advised that they both get out of town for a while. He suggested Vegas, so they could catch the Mayweather fight at the MGM Grand. They had the money to leave the city. Things were too hot in New York for them both. They had a high bounty on their heads, and the streets were crawling with enemies. K'wan was leery and felt that Vegas was too hot. Too many New York niggas could be there in the mix, but somehow Dwayne, who was hard-pressed to see a Mayweather fight, had convinced him otherwise. Once they arrived in Vegas, they planned to settle into a hotel suite, gamble, and relax.

With it still dark out, the trio made their way to Kennedy Airport in Queens. Paquitta had booked an early flight out of JFK to Vegas, and so far everything was going smoothly.

The Benz traveled toward Queens, taking Linden Boulevard. With it being early morning, the traffic was light. Mostly everything was still closed. Between the brothers, they carried ten thousand dollars apiece.

"Baby, you okay?" K'wan asked his girlfriend. She seemed too quiet, looking distant.

"I'm fine," Paquitta answered faintly.

"I know it's a setback now, baby," K'wan said. "But we gonna bounce fo' a minute, let things cool down, and come back to this town wit' a fuckin' vengeance. You hear me, baby? I got this."

"I hear you, baby," she replied. She stared out the window as the car traveled to the airport. She seemed to have a lot on her mind.

Tears leaked from her eyes and trickled down her face. She sighed, wiping away her tears and said to K'wan, "Baby, I love you."

K'wan smiled. "I know, baby."

"And I will always love you," she added.

The Benz came to a stop at a red light. K'wan and Dwayne looked befuddled by her sudden emotions.

"You okay, Paquitta?" Dwayne asked.

"I will never be okay after this," she responded.

The brothers were confused. They had no idea what she was talking about.

Out of the blue, Paquitta pulled out a pistol and fired. The gunshot was deafening inside the car. The bullet hit K'wan in the back of his head, and his blood splattered everywhere. He was forcefully thrust forward into the dashboard from the impact.

"Oh shit!" Dwayne shouted, wide-eyed.

He reached for his pistol, but Paquitta was already aiming at him. She shot a round point-blank into his face, and he went flying backwards into the driver's side window, spider-webbing the glass. His flesh and blood was coated all over the place too.

Paquitta hollered from the shooting she committed. The car went rolling forward and jumped the curb. She quickly got out and took a deep breath.

Both brothers were slumped in the front seat of the car, dead.

Paquitta cried loudly, the smoking gun still in her hand. She didn't have a choice. World had reached out to her with an offer she couldn't refuse—death to the brothers and a $100,000 payday or refuse and her babies and mother would be murdered. Paquitta had no idea how World found her, but since K'wan didn't trust anyone but Dwayne and her, it was the perfect setup.

Paquitta stumbled for a moment and then took off running, dropping the gun down a storm drain. Her life would never be the same. She loved K'wan, but his death was inevitable. They used the woman he loved and who loved him to pull the trigger. It was the way World wanted it. It would be the last hit he ordered.

***

Luca wanted to send her cousin home in style. His death came as expected, and she wanted to have a funeral for him that was fit for a king. It was ironic though. World was a murderous psychopath who'd killed dozens of people, yet his death was peaceful. He didn't go out in a hail of bullets.

"It's crazy, right, cuz? All the shit I did out there, the lives I took, and a nigga go out like this, sick and shit," World had said to her on his deathbed.

Luca held his hand as they talked.

World's funeral was in Brooklyn, where he grew up. Hundreds of people lined the streets to pay their respect as the funeral procession went through his old neighborhood. His body was displayed in a dark brushed bronze casket with bronze finish and premium velvet interior. He was dressed in a gray three-piece Armani suit and decorated with expensive jewelry.

He was carried through crowded streets by a horse-drawn carriage trailed by fourteen Rolls Royce limousines and was attended by many gangsters and a few Brooklyn celebrities that heard of World or grew up with him. Onlookers lined the streets to watch the procession, which traveled for blocks, from Pitkin Avenue, down Rockaway Avenue, and through the projects, ending at the church. There were so many people out in the streets, it looked like Biggie had died all over again.

So many people were appalled that the service of a psychotic killer and drug lord was allowed to take place at all. Many residents and political officials didn't want their city to be known for honoring a drug lord and thought it was a slap in the face, but Luca made sure the proper permits for the event had been filed.

***

After World's funeral, it was back to business. With his and her crews both paying allegiance to her, Luca was on top of the world. With World dead, she repackaged Bad Boy and Bad Girl. She began buying coke. Cocaine was now Bad Boy, and heroin was Bad Girl, so as to not confuse the clientele.

Luca was happy, pregnant, and her life was better than ever. Her foes were gone, besides Maribel and Angel in the wind somewhere. Luca hadn't heard their names or seen them around lately. She figured they'd wised up and decided to let bygones be bygones.

She confided in Kevin that she was pregnant with another man's baby. At first, he seemed angry, but he forgave her and was willing to raise the baby as his own child. They got engaged, and even though they'd fucked one time already, they agreed to wait until the baby was born to have sex again. He was still clueless to Luca's illegal activity.

Luca used Meeka as her contact to the streets. Everything and anything first went through Meeka, while Luca lived a quiet life, pregnant with a girl. She could see herself becoming a soccer mom, driving around in minivans with TEC-9s and assault rifles hidden in the back, ki's of cocaine in hidden compartments. Maybe she could open up a business and go legit one day.

***

Her private doctor smiled at the loving couple and stated that the baby was healthy. She was definitely a girl, and Luca was carrying her pregnancy well. Kevin stood by her side, holding her hand as she was being checked out. She was taking her prenatal pills regularly and living well.

"Are you guys excited?" the female doctor asked them.

"Very," Luca answered.

"We are," Kevin replied, smiling.

Kevin gleamed as he looked at the sonogram of his daughter on the monitor. Even though she wasn't biologically his daughter, he still felt like a proud, expecting father. He couldn't wait until Luca gave birth. He wanted to hold that beautiful infant girl in his arms and give her everything she needed.

Luca couldn't wait either. Finally, she was going to get what she always wanted, a baby, and having Kevin in her life was a major plus.

They up their visit with Dr. Trammell and walked out of the building joyously, holding hands. Kevin was doing great in school and trying to come up in the world, and Luca was there to help and encourage him.

It was another hot, summer day in Brooklyn. The borough was teeming with people and traffic. The only thing Luca wanted to do was go home and rest, and have Kevin massage her feet and back. He loved pleasing her. Whatever she needed, he didn't hesitate. If he had to make a run to the store in the middle of the night because she was craving something, then he did it.

Luca and Kevin walked to their car holding hands, talking and laughing like they always did.

Unbeknownst to Luca, her past was about to catch up to her. The looming threat followed them from behind, keenly watching her every movement.

When they got to the their little hooptie, something Kevin had saved for months for and bought, Kevin reached out to open the door for her, but then something caught his attention.

Out of nowhere sprung Maribel and her family. Maribel came charging at them wielding a razor.

Kevin tried to come in between the threat, but he found himself suddenly restrained by Maribel's father.

"You fuckin' bitch!" Maribel screamed heatedly.

Luca, caught off guard, felt the razor tear into her face. Her blood spewed, and she screamed frantically, feeling her flesh being torn away.

Kevin looked on in horror as Maribel repeatedly tore into his fiancée's face with the razor. "Nooo! Get off of her!" he screamed out.

He was being held back by Maribel's father, who was stronger and outweighed him by seventy pounds.

Rebecca jumped in and attacked Luca, while Maribel's father and cousins jumped Kevin, punching, kicking, and stomping him into the ground.

"I fuckin' told you, don't fuck wit' me, bitch! I told you I would be back! You can't hide from me!" Maribel shouted.

The assault was quick and vicious. When someone screamed out they were calling 9-1-1, Maribel and her family took off running.

Luca was crying out hysterically, worrying about her baby, her face cut open and coated with blood. She grabbed her protruding stomach and couldn't move.

Kevin saw the assault as an unprovoked attack on them. He didn't know any better, but Luca did, and every last one of them was going to pay with their lives.

They were rushed to the nearest hospital and treated. The good news was that her baby was fine; the bad news was her face was going to be scarred for life.

With her face being stitched together by doctors, looking like a Chucky doll, Luca was devastated. She was caught slipping and left herself open for attack. Now, the only thing that could make her happy was the slaughter of Maribel and her family. But she wanted to give them a slow, agonizing death.

When Meeka got word about the attack, she immediately came to Luca's aid. While Kevin was away talking to the doctors and trying to get other things situated, Luca, her face bandaged up like a mummy, talked to Meeka secretly, and put out a one-million-dollar contract on Maribel and her family.

"I'm on it, Luca. And we gonna find these muthafuckas and take care of them nice and slow, best believe that," Meeka assured her boss.

Luca knew Meeka wouldn't disappoint her. She had her crew scattered around the five boroughs and beyond, searching for the family.

Two weeks later, Meeka came back with word to Luca that Maribel and her entire family had fled the country. They had packed their things and moved back to Puerto Rico. Luca knew it was just a matter of time before they crept back into the States, and she was prepared to wait patiently.

Epilogue

Months later, Luca was living a seemingly normal life with Kevin, who still had no idea he was married to a vicious drug queenpin. They purchased a modest house in New Jersey, and Luca helped him open a McDonald's franchise on the New Jersey Turnpike.

She gave birth to a beautiful baby girl, 7lbs 9ounces, with a head full of curly black hair that she named, Lucky. Kevin was so in love with the new baby and his new bride. Thank God she looked like her mother and not Clyde.

The only upset to Luca was the scars. She was having consultations with the best plastic surgeons. It would take some time to fully heal. What hurt the most was, she had allowed a seventeen-year-old ghetto bitch to get the best of her when she'd gone up against kingpins, judges, cops, killers, lawyers, friends, the streets, and even her own family.

***

On Luca's 25th birthday, Kevin threw his wife a party with only family and some close friends. None of her associates were there. It was a private affair. She made it to see a quarter of a century. Luca felt proud that she managed to keep her business and private life completely separate.

The two-layer strawberry cake had her picture on it with the number 25 candle on top. Luca held her baby girl in her arms and smiled at the attention she was receiving.

After everyone sang happy birthday to her, she made a wish and blew out the candle.

"What you wish for, baby?" Kevin asked.

"Now you know I can't tell you that," Luca replied, smiling. "But I feel it already came through."

Luca's grandmother pulled her aside. "I'm proud of you, Luca. I'm glad you changed your life around. I always knew you would. It's good to see you breaking that cycle."

Luca smiled. "Thank you, Grandma."

Deep inside, it hurt that she was lying to them all.

On the low Lucinda slipped her granddaughter a sealed envelope with her name on it.

Luca was surprised "Grandma, you giving me money?"

Lucinda smiled. "If I could afford it, I would. It's something else. I was asked to give you that on your twenty-fifth birthday."

"By who?"

Luca was puzzled by it, especially being from World. She took the letter and walked into her bedroom, placed Lucky into her crib, and started to read the letter:

Dear Cuzzo,

If you're still alive, then I made the right decision. For months I agonized with a strange illness that the doctors couldn't diagnose. That's what I told everyone. But the thing is, they did finally tell me what was killing me. I was being poisoned with a substance called ricin. Since I'm legally crazy, I told those muthafuckas I smoked the shit purposely, because I didn't give a fuck. And then I bounced. But each time you showed up and gave me a pack of cigarettes, I smoked that shit knowing what was inside. I'm crazy, cuz, but I'm not stupid.

I guess you wondering why would I allow you to murder me? And if I knew all along it was you, then why have K'wan murdered? You're a smart girl, Luca, and I'm sure you'd figure that out. But I'll tell you just in case your theory isn't in line with the truth. I had K'wan murdered because I knew that once I was dead, you wouldn't last but one week. K'wan would have murdered you and took over my organization. And for some strange reason, I wanted family to be my successor.

I feel you've earned your position on the throne. Luca, you did something I just couldn't do—murder my own blood. No matter how much I felt like it was easy being a drug kingpin, bodying muthafuckas without losing a wink of sleep, I could never kill you with my bare hands. That told me I really wasn't built for this, and that you, Luca, rightfully were. By the time the doctors figured out what happened, I was already dead.

I hope everything you've lost and gained from inception to now was worth it. I hope I didn't die in vain. I hope my little cousin is making bitches sick and niggas die for fuckin' with her. I hope you've proven once and for all that you're a bad girl.

World

Luca was stunned by the letter, but only momentarily. It was written just as crazy as he was. It didn't make sense, but World was unpredictable. She was poisoning him with ricin. When inhaled or injected, a few grains of it could kill an adult, but Luca made World's death gradual and painful, to make it look like he was dying from a disease.

She looked down at her baby, sleeping peacefully in her crib and then looked out her bedroom bay window and observed her family celebrating. Her husband was barbecuing by the grill, her grandmother was preaching to the young kids, and her mother was playing with the kids.

Luca sat at the foot of her bed and looked in thought about something. She reached over and picked up her cell phone from off the nightstand and made an important call.

Meeka answered, "Happy birthday, Luca."

Luca didn't even reply with a thank-you. "I want you to double the bounty on Maribel's head, and her family too. I want that bitch and her family dead before the weekend. And while you're at it, send Scotch and a couple of goons uptown to kill Angel. That bitch needs to go; take out the problem before it escalates."

"I'm on it, Luca."

"And my attorney, Dominic Sirocco, I want that nigga found and handled—not permanently, because I want to have a nice chat with him."

"On it," Meeka responded again.

Luca hung up and smiled. She was a bad girl, and Bad Girls do bad things.